Charlotte Cheetham: Master of Disaster

Charlotte Cheetham: Master of Disaster

by Barbara Ware Holmes

illustrated by
John Himmelman

c.2

HARPER & ROW, PUBLISHERS

Designed by Joyce Hopkins
2 3 4 5 6 7 8 9 10

Library of Congress Cataloging in Publication Data
Holmes, Barbara Ware.
  Charlotte Cheetham, master of disaster.

  Summary: Charlotte, a fifth grader who simply can
not keep from telling tall stories, tells her most
outlandish tale ever in her desperation to be
included by a group of girls in her class.
  1. Children's stories, American. [1. Honesty—
Fiction. 2. Schools—Fiction] I. Himmelman, John, ill.
II. Title.
PZ7.H7337Ch 1985   [Fic]   85-42617
ISBN 0-06-022587-4
ISBN 0-06-022588-2 (lib. bdg.)

for
SARAH ANNE HOLMES

The author wishes to express special thanks to
Mrs. Paula Goettelmann of Zane North School in
Collingswood, New Jersey,
whose fourth-grade students (1981–82)
became Charlotte's earliest champions.

Charlotte Cheetham: Master of Disaster

1

Charlotte Cheetham stared across the desk at the librarian. Mrs. Arnold had long blond hair and green eyes. Charlotte thought she must be the most beautiful woman in the world. Women in Charlotte's family were all dark haired with crooked teeth and nothing at all remarkable about them.

Mrs. Arnold smiled and handed Charlotte her book. "How are you, Charlotte?" she asked.

"Fine." Charlotte smiled back. "My mom had a baby last night." She watched Mrs. Arnold's green eyes widen in surprise. She felt mildly startled herself. There was no baby. The story had just popped, uninvited, into Charlotte's head. She had offered it to Mrs. Arnold as a reward for her interest.

"Really? Why, how nice. Was it a boy or a girl?" the librarian asked in the way she had of seeming interested in everything a person had to say.

"A boy," Charlotte said, suddenly picturing the rosy little thing wrapped in blankets with only his nose and squinty eyes showing. Under the blanket his skin would be all wrinkled and he'd probably have a rash, but that was okay. Babies were like little pink Kermits. They were supposed to be ugly.

"Does he have a name?" the librarian asked.

Charlotte nodded. "Bill," she said, the name popping into her head just as easily as the baby. "They named him Bill." He would sleep in the upstairs room her mother called a study, though no one ever studied there. She imagined a crib pushed against the wall with colorful cardboard fish swinging over it for Bill to gurgle at. The room would be blue, she decided. With rainbow stripes across the ceiling.

Mrs. Arnold's hand rested suddenly on Charlotte's shoulder as she bent across the desk to look closely into her face. "You tell your mother congratulations for me, all right, Charlotte?" Her eyes were kind and trusting. Charlotte felt a flush creep up her neck and onto her ears. She lowered her gaze to stare at the large blue buttons on Mrs. Arnold's sweater.

"Yes," she said weakly. "I will." She was sud-

2

denly overwhelmed with loss, sensing she could never look directly into those green eyes again.

She would hate to have a baby brother, she thought on the way back to her classroom. What had made her make up a terrible story like that?

The class was reading when Charlotte came back into her room. She handed her library pass to Miss Brown and smiled, holding her book close to her side so the teacher wouldn't notice it.

"How did you make out, Charlotte?" Miss Brown asked. The question sounded polite, but Charlotte knew it wasn't. It was a trick.

"Fine."

Miss Brown smiled. "Did you find an interesting book?"

Charlotte didn't answer. At this point she was supposed to hold up her book and say, "Oh, yes," and show her teacher what a good choice she'd made. She held her book pressed firmly to her side and stared at the brown blotter on Miss Brown's desk. She wondered if her teacher liked brown things because of her name. Looking down, she saw that Miss Brown wore brown shoes.

"Let me see, Charlotte," Miss Brown said firmly. Charlotte didn't move. Miss Brown reached down and took the book from her hand. "Oh, Charlotte." Charlotte hung her head. "What did I tell you?"

Charlotte sighed. "You told me to stop checking out only Pippi Longstocking books," she said sullenly. Her copy of *Pippi in the South Seas* now sat on the brown blotter. Miss Brown tapped her fingers on it without taking her eyes off Charlotte.

"So why did you come back with this?" she asked.

Charlotte wouldn't answer. It was a stupid question. The Pippi books were the only ones she liked. As long as one of them sat there in the library, how could she not come back with it?

"There are hundreds of good books in the library," Miss Brown persisted. "Doesn't Mrs. Arnold help you?"

Charlotte knew she would regret whatever words were about to come out of her mouth. "Mrs. Arnold says she understands why I like these books so much," she said angrily. "She says when she was a kid she only read Pippi books, too!" The flush crept along her neck again. The classroom was silent, everyone listening. She wished she hadn't worn her hair in braids so they could all see her ears.

Miss Brown sighed. "All right, Charlotte. But next time you're to select something else. Do you understand?" She handed the Pippi book to Charlotte. "Otherwise, you won't use the library at all."

And what was the point of using the library if she couldn't take out what she liked? Charlotte thought bitterly as she reached for the book. She refused to look her teacher in the eye. She hated Miss Brown. She'd made Charlotte tell a lie about Mrs. Arnold!

But the lie she'd just told seemed nothing compared to the one she'd come up with all on her own in the library, she admitted to herself as she made her way back to her seat. Her friend Annie was snickering behind the raised top of her desk. Charlotte fell into her chair, thinking there was not one person in the whole world who had any sense besides Mrs. Arnold, and now she'd lied to her.

The lie haunted Charlotte all morning, but she tried not to think about it. Whenever she felt it sneaking into her mind, she thought about the kitten instead. Charlotte was soon to be the owner of a small gray cat. She'd known that for weeks. Listening to Mrs. Pascal complain to her father, she'd had one of those feelings that can't be explained.

"Wild cats," Mrs. Pascal had said in disgust. "There were at least six of them under my porch. You should see what they've done to the garden!" Charlotte had listened with pleasure to the stories of what had happened to Mrs. Pascal's petunias and peonies. No one liked Mrs. Pascal. "We've caught most of them," the woman said. "There's one or two we can't get our hands on."

Charlotte had gone immediately to Mrs. Pascal's yard to investigate, but had found only squirrels. It wasn't until she began leaving bowls of milk beside the bushes that she spotted the little gray cat. They had stared at each other for a long time before the cat had dared to drink. Charlotte couldn't get close, but that was all right. It was only a matter of time.

Two things she'd known without being told. She was born to be the owner of that cat. And the cat's name was Pippi.

But it was no use. Having Pippi wouldn't change things. Charlotte would still be the same dumb person who'd lied to the librarian. She plopped wearily into a seat at the lunch table and stared, without interest, at her brown-bag lunch.

"You look sort of funny," Annie said, watching her.

Charlotte nodded.

"Are you sick?"

Charlotte shook her head and scowled into her lunch bag. Her sister Ruth had packed lunches last night. She could expect anything. Exploding

6

sandwiches. Bugs. Nails in her fruit.

"Are you mad at me?"

Charlotte glared across the table at Annie. When
you were depressed, you didn't want to talk about
it. Talking didn't cheer you up. Nothing did. But
the sight of Annie's gloomy face made her un-
comfortable. Charlotte sighed again and examined her sandwich. Cheese. Plain old cheese on
plain brown bread. Boring, just like her sister.
Ruth would never think of exploding sandwiches.

"No," she said to Annie. "I'm not mad at you."
Annie smiled and took a bite of her own sandwich. Peanut butter and jelly, Charlotte saw. Same
old thing. Same old Annie. Charlotte knew she'd
neglected her friend lately, spending all her time
carrying bowls of milk back and forth to the Pascals' bushes. But Pippi would never come out if

two of them were there. It wasn't that she didn't *like* Annie anymore. She just couldn't hang around with her after school. Why did Annie have to be so mopey about it?

"Maybe you can come to my house today," Charlotte said grudgingly. If Annie went home by five o'clock, she could still run milk over to Pippi before her parents got home. Annie stopped chewing and beamed a surprised smile at her.

"But *not* for dinner." Annie's smile dimmed, but she nodded. Annie loved eating at Charlotte's house. She thought it was interesting when Charlotte's mother discussed her research—who did what to the little white mice at the lab today. She laughed when Charlotte's father, the art teacher, said he could only digest complementary colors. Charlotte had heard that one a million times. Annie acted like *any*thing was worth listening to, even if Ruth or Marie said it. Personally, Charlotte thought dinner at Annie's house, with just a quiet, ordinary mother, was perfect bliss. Nobody talked. Nobody told corny jokes.

"Can we play pool?" Annie asked, her eyes bright.

Pool? Charlotte couldn't think of a single thing she'd like to do less, but she nodded. Tomorrow Annie was going to have to go back to moping. Charlotte hoped to cram two or three weeks' worth of niceness into one afternoon.

8

2

"I'll trade you this Smurf for that puffy," Tina said to Laura. "The big one." Even from across the room, Charlotte could smell a rat. She frowned and shook her head at Laura.

"Cut it out, Charlotte," Tina said, seeing her. "Mind your own business."

Charlotte bent over her spelling. "Cheater," she muttered, but Tina and Laura didn't notice. They'd gone back to passing stickers back and forth across the table, fingering them as if they were gold and not just something cheap and ordinary you could buy in any drugstore.

Charlotte sighed. How was she supposed to concentrate with them in here? She'd been ordered to stay inside at recess every day for a week and correct her spelling papers. Spelling made her angry. It wasn't that she didn't know how to spell—she just got bored with words the way they were. She didn't see why they always had to be spelled the same way. And she hated staying in for recess. That was what failures had to do. Charlotte pretended to herself that she'd been called inside to write an important document. She was writing a speech for Miss Brown to deliver at the next PTA meeting. It was about how interesting children liked to spell words differently. "Teacher," for instance, could also be "teecher." Or even "teechim" if you were teaching boys. Charlotte smiled.

"How about this?" Laura said to Tina. "Skunk. Smell."

Skunk? Charlotte looked up.

"They make stickers that smell like skunk?" she asked, crossing the room to investigate. Laura waved the sticker beneath her nose. It did smell like skunk. Phew! Charlotte was impressed.

"I'll trade you this for that," Tina was saying now, pointing to a large fuzzy sticker of a dog that took up half a page in Laura's book. She was offering a large round sticker with a dove in the center.

"Don't do it," Charlotte said to Laura. The sticker, however, was already trading hands. Charlotte bristled as she saw the dog take its place in Tina's book. Tina always got everything good.

"That was a rip-off," she said to Laura. "You shouldn't have traded that."

Tina and Laura paused in their dealings to look up at her. "What do you know?" Tina said. "You don't even have stickers."

"I know a rip-off when I see one," Charlotte said stubbornly. But they were not interested. They went back to the business of trading, oblivious to her.

Charlotte watched a while longer, jealous of the way their eyes and hands traveled the table making deals that did not include her. And Tina was getting all the good ones.

"Who wants stickers, anyway?" Charlotte said, thinking that *she* did. Tina was flipping slowly through the pages of her album in search of a trade and didn't reply. She had hundreds of stickers, Charlotte saw. Maybe thousands.

"Good trees were cut down to make those stickers," she pointed out. "What a waste." When there was still no reply, Charlotte watched the pages flick by and studied the perfectly straight part in Tina's shiny dark-brown hair. Charlotte had made her own braids this morning: one thick and one thin.

"Gum trees," she continued. They had just studied gum trees in their unit on Australia. Not gum as in bubble gum, Miss Brown had ex-

11

plained. Gum as in glue. Charlotte had thought such trees a wonderful invention—both the glue and the paper right there. If she were a person who made stickers or Contact paper, she would live in Australia.

"Gum trees?" Tina looked up at last, the pages of her album stilled.

"That's right," Charlotte said triumphantly. In her mind, acres of barren gum-tree stumps now dotted the Australian landscape. She paused to smile at several girls returning noisily to class, witnesses to Tina's rapidly approaching downfall.

"Think of the koalas," she said in outrage, imagining little bears clinging forlornly to treeless stumps. She noted, with satisfaction, that looks of amazement had spread across Tina's and Laura's faces. The other girls moved closer.

"The koalas?" Tina said, staring at Laura, obviously at a loss for words. Or maybe she didn't understand.

"Of course," Charlotte said patiently. The acres of gum-tree stumps had expanded in her mind to cover the entire continent of Australia. And it *could* happen—after all, there used to be trees and wigwams where there was now New Jersey. "You kill gum trees, you kill koalas," she explained, watching Tina's face for signs of shame.

The expression expanding across Tina's face was not guilt, however, but glee. "Koalas?" she repeated, her voice a squeal that fell off into laughter—long, loud gales of laughter that left her holding her sides and gasping for breath. Charlotte stared at her in disbelief. Everyone else had begun to laugh also.

"She thinks they're made from gum trees," Laura squeaked, swiping at her eyes and looking wildly into Charlotte's face. The laughter seemed loud enough to be heard three rooms away. Charlotte sensed people on the playground bending to look in the windows. Humiliated, she tore from the room.

"Charlotte, where's your spelling?" Miss Brown asked when recess was over.

"I got distracted," Charlotte said, eyeing Tina, who smirked at her. Miss Brown went red with anger.

"I also had to write a speech," she hastened to add, but Miss Brown did not look impressed. Her face resembled a red balloon about to burst. Charlotte stared at her in awe. Even *she* couldn't turn *that* red.

"If I tell you to stay inside to do spelling," the teacher said loudly, "then you stay inside and do spelling." Charlotte had never seen her look so angry. She began to grow alarmed. Behind her, the class was still. "You never, ever, do what I ask, Charlotte. Not *ever*. Have you noticed that?"

Charlotte hung her head. She felt all eyes upon her. "I mean to," she said honestly. "Things just don't seem to work out." She heard snickers from the back of the classroom. Tina. This was all her fault.

"I suggest they start working out," Miss Brown said. "Today you're going to stay after school and do spelling again. If you have to, you'll stay after school every day for the rest of the year. Now sit down."

Charlotte sat, hearing the snickers grow louder

14

behind her. Creep, she thought, knowing it was Tina. She closed her eyes and concentrated, trying to ESP a disaster in the back of the room. The light on the ceiling would fall on Tina's head. Miraculously, no one else would be hurt, except for Laura, perhaps, who would suffer minor cuts and abrasions. Charlotte waited, but nothing happened. She believed in her ESP; it just never worked.

To her relief, Tina and Laura were finally called to the corner of the room for reading. "The Unicorns," the group had named itself. Tina had provided each of them with a unicorn sticker for the front of his workbook. Unicorns! Charlotte thought scornfully. *Puny*-corns was more like it. Thinking of Tina as a puny-corn made Charlotte feel better.

"Charlotte, would you please come up here a moment?" Miss Brown said when she had settled the group into their corner for silent reading.

Charlotte approached Miss Brown's desk nervously, thinking of all the things she'd done to upset her in one day. She was going to get it. Sure enough, Miss Brown's face pulled itself into its Lecture Look. Charlotte hoped the teacher would at least manage to keep her voice down. She'd had enough embarrassment for one day.

"You know, Charlotte," Miss Brown began in

15

a surprisingly quiet voice, "according to the Iowa tests, you read on the seventh-grade level." She waited for this pronouncement to sink in. Charlotte wondered what she was supposed to say. Was it a crime to read on the seventh-grade level if you were only in the fifth grade? Maybe it ruined Miss Brown's records.

When Charlotte didn't reply, the Lecture Look grew firmer. "You should be in the top reading group, with Tina and Laura and Robert. Do you have any idea why you're not?"

Charlotte nodded. "I don't do my workbooks," she said. And she never would if it would keep her from becoming a puny-corn.

"And so you get Cs in reading," Miss Brown continued. Charlotte wondered how she managed to talk and keep her mouth so firmly set. "It would take you fifteen minutes a day to do your workbooks. You could do them with half your brain, Charlotte. They're very simple."

"Well, I know," Charlotte agreed. "They just ask you what happened in the stories. How can I not know what happened in fifth-grade stories if I read on the seventh-grade level? They're dumb." Miss Brown's firm look turned to something resembling Jell-O.

"But I don't mind getting Cs," Charlotte said, trying to sound pleasant. In fact, Cs seemed to

16

her a fair trade for escaping Tina's reading group. Miss Brown, however, had pulled herself together and the Lecture Look reappeared.

"The workbooks are for *me*, Charlotte. So that *I* know you comprehended the stories. And you *should* mind getting Cs if you're capable of As. You have no self-discipline. Now go to your seat and take out the workbook for the last story you read."

Who needed self-discipline? Charlotte thought wearily on the way back to her desk. It seemed to her the rest of the world had enough discipline to hold her down forever.

3

It was four o'clock that afternoon before Charlotte finished her workbook and her spelling and was allowed to leave school. She walked dejectedly, staring at her feet and kicking stones ahead of her. Maybe she would take this week's allowance and buy some stickers, she thought to cheer herself up. She'd spend all her allowances for the next five years on stickers.

"I'll have hundreds, too," she announced, aiming a rock so that it slammed into another, several feet away. She would keep them in big red albums like Tina's that her mother would buy for her. Mrs. Cheetham approved of collections when she thought things would end up labeled and organized.

The trouble was, every time Charlotte carried

a dollar to the drugstore to start her sticker collection, the stickers didn't interest her a dollar's worth. There were so many other things she'd rather have. Comic books, for instance. Or Garfield erasers. She was a sucker for anything with Garfield on it. She admitted it.

Besides, there were too many things in the world to collect. If she decided on rocks, she'd start noticing seashells. There were postcards and posters and coins and bubble-gum cards and stamps, all of them interesting. She'd never managed to put together a real collection of anything.

She sighed and stopped walking so she could think more clearly. One thing stickers definitely had in their favor—they were popular. Charlotte thought that if she had books and books of them, some of their popularity would have to spill over onto her.

"Charlotte? What are you doing?" Charlotte looked up to see Annie at the corner, watching her think. She realized that one of her hands was in midair, as if she'd been gesturing to herself. Maybe even talking out loud, though she didn't recollect hearing the sound of her voice recently.

"Nothing," she said, embarrassed. She dropped her hand.

"We're supposed to play," Annie said sullenly, coming to meet her. Annie didn't seem to notice

19

when Charlotte did embarrassing things. Charlotte wondered if there was something wrong with her. "How come you didn't do your spelling at recess, anyway?"

The thought of spelling and recess made Charlotte's feet move again. "I didn't feel like it," she said, sensing Annie close behind her as she set off toward home.

"Boy, was the teacher mad," Annie said with a touch of awe.

"The teacher's always mad," Charlotte pointed out. "I hate school. I might quit."

Annie laughed loudly, but with appreciation. "How about playing now?" she asked, hurrying to keep up with Charlotte.

But Charlotte had stopped, preoccupied again, this time bending down and peering into the bushes that lined the Pascals' driveway and bordered their yard.

"What are you looking for?" Annie demanded, her patience wearing thin. "What are you doing?"

Charlotte straightened up and began walking again. "Nothing," she said. Beside her, Annie was silent.

"You never tell me anything anymore," Annie said finally as they approached the corner where they usually parted. Her voice was shaky with unhappiness. "And you can never play. I waited an *hour* for you today!"

20

Charlotte flushed. She had forgotten all about Annie. Not that she could help being late. "I had to stay after school," she said defensively. "That wasn't my fault. And I can't help having secrets. Something secret just came along."

Annie's face, when she dared glance at it, had darkened ominously. Charlotte couldn't tell if she was going to burst into tears or throw her books at the ground. Annie herself seemed undecided.

"You're weird, Charlotte Cheetham," she flung out finally, turning to spit the words at Charlotte. "Everyone says so. I don't know why I play with you. Being weird might rub off!" And she left, trailing papers and the belt to her dress.

"It doesn't matter," Charlotte told herself, slowly walking the last block to her house. Annie was the kind of friend who had to know everything about every minute of your life.

"Who needs that?" Charlotte said aloud to no one in particular. The words made her feel slightly better. "Who needs that?" she repeated. And who cared if everyone thought she was weird? But her arms and legs suddenly felt so heavy she could hardly drag them through the backyard into her house.

"Hi, ugly," Charlotte's sister Marie said when she came into the kitchen. Charlotte scowled and didn't reply. No wonder she was weird. Just living with her sisters made strange thoughts come

21

into her head and out her mouth.

"Mom says do your homework and set the table before she comes home."

Charlotte nodded. She spread her books out on the kitchen table as if she were preparing to do her homework and waited for her sister to leave the kitchen.

In the living room, Marie turned on the television set and settled down in front of it. Ruth was at soccer practice. Quietly, carefully, Charlotte opened the refrigerator and took out the milk carton. She filled a small pink plastic bowl and returned the carton to the refrigerator.

She supposed she looked silly carrying the bowl through the backyard and down the street to the Pascals' house. Weird. She sighed and her lower lip quivered. The milk in the bowl sloshed precariously.

"Here, Pippi," she called softly when she'd arrived at the bushes. She set the dish far enough back from the sidewalk that it wouldn't be seen. "Come on, Pippi." Charlotte knew the cat wouldn't come until she'd backed away, but she was certain it was nearby, listening.

Sure enough, when Charlotte had moved off a few feet, a small gray cat appeared. It stopped, as it always did, to watch Charlotte for a long minute. Charlotte was careful to be absolutely still. Finally the cat approached the bowl and began to drink, her eyes turned up to look at Charlotte while her tongue lapped furiously at the milk. She didn't stop drinking until the bowl was empty.

"You were hungry today," Charlotte said. She wanted the animal to grow used to her voice. The cat sat down and stared at her. It began to lick its paws and wash its face. Charlotte edged a little closer. The cat stopped with its paw in the air and watched her. "I'm your friend," Charlotte said. "Good Pippi." But when she moved another inch, Pippi bolted.

Charlotte felt abandoned. "Dumb cat," she said into the bushes, trying to sound like someone who was not about to cry. "I'm going to be an adult before you come to live with me. I might not even want you then!" The bushes were still.

"Dumb cat," she said again as she carried the

bowl home. But she didn't mean it. She was afraid for the cat. It occurred to her suddenly that in taming Pippi she was making it easier for Mrs. Pascal to catch her. Charlotte's heart pounded in fear.

"Oh, Pippi," she said aloud. "You better start liking me in a hurry."

But it didn't seem likely that Pippi would ever start liking Charlotte Cheetham. Why should she? No one else did.

Charlotte had two dollars and eighty-five cents. She turned the old rubber boot she used for a bank upside down and watched the nickels and quarters roll across the bedspread. Two dollars and eighty-five cents. She wondered how many stickers that would buy. If she hurried, she could set the table and make it to the drugstore before dinner, she thought, gathering up the coins.

This time the stickers looked more interesting. She hadn't known about scratch-and-sniffs. She lifted each sheet to her nose, trying to smell the stickers through the plastic they were packaged in. She could smell the soap ones that smelled like her mother's detergent. Who would buy those? The others just smelled like plastic.

"Can I help you, Charlotte?" Mr. Sutphen asked, coming up behind her. Mr. Sutphen owned the

drugstore. Charlotte was embarrassed to be caught sniffing his merchandise.

"These are scratch-and-sniff stickers," she explained. "When you scratch them, they smell."

Mr. Sutphen smiled. He reached behind her to pull out a large sheet of cardboard with all the stickers displayed on it. "Here," he said. "Samples."

Excited, Charlotte took the cardboard and began to scratch the stickers, being careful not to scratch so hard that Mr. Sutphen would think she was wearing the smell out of them.

She saw the one she wanted immediately. Old shoes! The sticker smelled just like the shoes her father wore to cut the grass. Charlotte always seemed to end up lying next to them on the rug when she watched TV. "Gross," she said elatedly.

The old shoes came in a package with rotten eggs and tennis balls. Mr. Sutphen laughed aloud when she pointed it out. She also chose a sheet of fuzzy cats, one of which looked exactly like Pippi. She would never trade that one, she thought, reaching into her boot for her change.

4

"How's Baby Bill?" her sister Marie asked at dinner. Everyone looked up, curious, except Charlotte, who tried to shrink into the kind of person too small and unimportant-looking to be noticed.

"Who's Baby Bill?" Mrs. Cheetham asked, dropping more carrots onto Charlotte's plate. Charlotte didn't dare complain.

"You don't know?" Marie said innocently. "You had a baby last night and don't even remember?"

Mrs. Cheetham looked impatient. "Whatever kind of joke that is, it's not funny."

Marie and Ruth, Charlotte's oldest sister, giggled. Charlotte felt as if her shoes were filled with rocks and pulling the rest of her under the table.

"Sit up, Charlotte," Mrs. Cheetham said. "Eat. You, too," she said to Marie. "No more jokes."

Marie smiled happily. "It's not a joke," she said. "Our librarian said to give you her congratulations. She said we sure were lucky to have such a large family." She and Ruth began to giggle again, uncontrollably. "She said it's amazing how you do all you do."

Mrs. Cheetham looked at her husband and back again at the girls. "Come on, now," she said. "What's going on?"

Marie glanced at Charlotte. "Charlotte told Mrs. Arnold you'd had a baby named Bill."

"My," Mr. Cheetham said into the silence that followed this pronouncement, "you *have* been busy." He nodded in the direction of his startled wife. Charlotte hung her head.

"Charlotte?" Her mother's voice was full of dismay instead of anger. Charlotte started to cry, big tears that dropped off her cheeks into the carrots on her plate. "Why on earth would you say a thing like that?" her mother asked. "How could you tell a lie to your librarian?"

Charlotte tried to say she was sorry, but sobs rose up and burst from her mouth when she opened it to speak. Her family sat in silence while she made gulping and gasping sounds and pulled at the ends of her braids. Part of her thought it felt good to be gushing forth tears after a humiliating day, but the other part was conscious

of her sisters, who were watching her behave like a baby.

"It's a serious thing," her mother said, when Charlotte had finally run out of tears. She was making gulping noises that felt like hiccups. The carrots inside her seemed to be bouncing against her ribs. "You can't go around telling people anything you'd like and leaving them to believe it. Mrs. Arnold actually thinks you have a baby brother."

"No, she doesn't," Marie said. "I told her Charlotte was lying. I told her she always lies."

Charlotte wished right then that her mother had killed her once and for all, or that she'd choke to death on carrots. She began to cry again, tears appearing, miraculously, from somewhere.

"Why don't you go upstairs, Charlotte," her mother suggested. "You're going to make yourself sick if you try to eat now. And you think things over."

Upstairs, Charlotte lay facedown on her bed and thought things over. Lying wasn't the worst thing in the world, she decided. It wasn't as bad as being mean. And besides, she wasn't really lying. She always believed the stories when she was telling them. Maybe she was just crazy. She sat up to consider this. Being crazy and weird wasn't her fault. She wondered if Mrs. Arnold would forgive her if she explained that she was crazy. But the thought of walking into the library sent goose bumps down her spine, and Charlotte knew she couldn't do it. She would have to avoid Mrs. Arnold for the rest of her life.

It was only a matter of time, of course, before Mrs. Cheetham appeared at the door of Charlotte's room to have a Serious Talk. A Serious Talk meant that her mother was going to try to be nice when she really felt like screaming. Sometimes, Charlotte would rather be screamed at than sit through one of her mother's talks.

"I just want you to know that I understand," her mother began. Charlotte looked at her suspiciously. This was a new kind of beginning for a Serious Talk. It sounded more like something her father would say. "I know you don't think you're lying when you tell stories. And in a way, you're not. I mean I don't suppose you lie when your father and I ask you a question about something." An uncertain look passed through her mother's eyes, and Charlotte thought the statement was really a question.

"No," Charlotte offered. "I don't do that." *Too* often, she added silently.

Her mother nodded. "Your stories are just— little adventures you like to create for yourself, I guess. And for you, for a little while, they're real. So it isn't really lying."

Charlotte considered it. "Yeah," she said brightly, looking at her mother with a new respect. "I guess that's what I do."

"But you can't just go around telling your stories and having everyone think they're true. It isn't fair to other people. Do you understand?"

Charlotte nodded her head slowly, but her insides were saying, "No." It was all right to make up adventures, but not to tell them? When she told them she was usually still believing them. The only way to stop herself would be to just not talk.

"You're ten years old," her mother was continuing. Charlotte no longer liked the way her voice was sounding. Her words were trying to impress Charlotte with how old she was now, but her voice was saying she was still a baby. Her kindergarten teacher had talked like that.

31

Mrs. Arnold was the only grown-up who never spoke to kids that way. Charlotte felt weak with sadness that she would never see the librarian again.

"People won't be able to trust you," her mother said. "They'll never know if you're telling the truth or lying."

Charlotte's sadness dissolved into anger. Now her mother was calling it lying. Was it or wasn't it? She looked at her mother with distrust. She watched her crooked teeth move up and down as she talked, and studied the dark-brown hair that was pulled back into a knot like an old person's. Her mother was hopeless, Charlotte thought. Why should she even listen to what she had to say? She was ugly and dull and—worst of all—she was a scientist who worked in a lab with rats and mice. Charlotte hated going into the lab where it smelled funny and all the people wore glasses and never looked directly at her. If they did, she felt like a mouse about to get zapped.

It wasn't fair. Kids should get to vote on what parents they got. If she were Mrs. Arnold's daughter, she would never tell lies. Someone that beautiful and kind and normal could never have a crazy person for a kid.

Her mother had continued saying things Charlotte didn't hear.

"All right?" she was asking seriously, leaning forward to look Charlotte in the eye. Charlotte nodded, against her will. Sometimes she suspected her mother could hypnotize her. Make her say anything.

"Fine." Her mother kissed her on the head and stood up. "You're a little monkey," she said and left.

Charlotte scratched her armpits like a monkey in the direction of the closed door and stuck out her tongue for good measure.

"You're too creative for your own good, Charlotte," Mr. Cheetham said softly when he came in later to kiss her good night. "I know a little about that myself."

33

Charlotte wondered if he was talking about those pictures he drew of people with no clothes on. They'd probably gotten him into a lot of trouble.

"You have to find a way to channel all that creativity into something positive. You know? Master your talents."

Charlotte nodded, though she didn't, really. She hadn't inherited any of her father's talent for drawing, if that was what he meant. She wasn't particularly good at anything. A master of disaster, that was about it. Besides, "channeling creativity" sounded a lot like having self-discipline. She wished everybody would just leave her alone and let her be depressed in peace.

5

"Hey, I didn't know you had stickers," Annie said the next morning, seeing the stickers poking out of the top of Charlotte's school bag. They had met up at the corner as usual, neither of them wanting to remember their angry parting of the day before.

"I just got them," Charlotte said, trying to be likeable. "At the drugstore. You should buy some and we could trade."

Annie looked interested. "What kind did you get?" she asked, pulling out one of the packages.

Charlotte, whose insides always bubbled with irritation when Annie reached into her bag, tried to smile. Annie had her nose in the open package, sniffing.

"Shoes and rotten eggs?" she said, smiling at Charlotte. "Neat."

Charlotte nodded and stuck the stickers back into her bag, alongside her Pippi book. Annie, watching, now reached in and pulled out the book.

"Why do you like these books so much, anyway?" she asked. "Pippi's weird. She keeps a horse on her porch and garbage all over her house. You'd get a disease living in a place like that. Besides, nobody lets nine-year-olds live by themselves. It's dumb."

Charlotte grabbed the book out of Annie's hand. She thought the top of her head might blow off, but she didn't reply.

"You should read Judy Blume books," Annie said earnestly. "They're about *real* things. There's even one about getting your period."

"I would *never* read a Judy Blume book," Charlotte said more loudly and dramatically than she'd intended. "And I'm not taking *any* books out of the library. Ever. For as long as I live and go to that school. I'll die first." She slid *Pippi in the South Seas* back into her bag and slapped it closed.

Annie was silenced by her outburst. Charlotte, relieved to have finally said something outrageous, began to think clearly. She realized that Miss Brown, in forbidding her to take out Pippi books, had provided her with the perfect excuse for avoiding the library. Charlotte smiled to herself.

"You can take my book back for me when you go," she said to Annie. "If you don't mind, that is." She smiled agreeably and linked arms with her friend.

Annie smiled, too. She didn't mind at all.

"I have some stickers," Charlotte said to Tina at lunchtime. "Want to trade?"

Tina didn't look up. She took a bite of her peanut-butter sandwich. "I don't know," she said. "Depends on what they are."

"Scratch-and-sniffs and fuzzies," Charlotte said. Annie, across the table, was the only one who seemed to be listening with any real interest. "Old shoes," Charlotte added. "And tennis balls."

"Have 'em," Tina said. She and Jenny were busy trying to stomp on Laura's feet. Laura giggled and swung her legs wildly beneath the table.

"Well, you won't believe the stickers I'm going to have soon," Charlotte said loudly. Tina glanced at her and made a dash for Laura's shoe again.

"Oh yeah? Like what?"

Charlotte shrugged. "Kinds you have never heard of in your life," she said, trying to sound mysterious.

All three of them paused in their scrambling to laugh. "Sure, Charlotte," Laura said.

"I thought you hated stickers," Tina said, suddenly taking interest. "What about all those little koala bears?" She and Laura giggled.

Charlotte blushed. She thought that being a liar was nothing compared to being a rat like Tina. "I do hate them," she said. "I didn't buy these." Across the table, Annie's eyes widened. "I was *forced* to take them. And I'll have to take hundreds more, because the person who gave them to me owns a factory that makes them."

Tina rolled her eyes. "Give me a break," she said.

"It's true," Charlotte insisted. "She's a friend of my mother's, and she owns a sticker factory." Her mother knew hundreds of important people. She might very well know the owner of a sticker factory.

"You are so full of it, Charlotte, I can't believe my ears," Tina said. Laura and Jenny chuckled.

Charlotte sat up angrily. The other kids were always challenging her. It wasn't fair. How did they know her mother didn't have a friend in the sticker business? To Charlotte, the friend seemed suddenly very real. "Well I'm going up there," she said, leaning close to Tina's mocking face. "To see the factory. I don't even want to, because stickers are so boring, but I *have* to. I'll have so many stickers I'll have to throw them away."

Everyone was looking at her, beginning to believe. Charlotte felt a tiny glow of victory. "You can come if you want to," she said, fanning the glow into a full-fledged fire.

"What?" Tina said, surprised. "To the factory?" She leaned away from Charlotte. Eagerness began to play across her face. "Is this for real, Charlotte?"

Charlotte clicked her tongue in exasperation. "How could I invite you someplace that didn't exist?" she said.

Tina and Laura looked at each other.

"When?" Tina said.

"Weekend after next, in New York City. You can all come if you want," Charlotte added generously.

Laura's eyes were bright. "Really?" she said. "Swear to God you aren't making this up?"

Charlotte nodded her head.

"Wow," Laura said. "Thanks."

"You told me you got those stickers at the drugstore," Annie said when the girls had gone outside to play. "How come you didn't tell *me* about the factory?"

Charlotte felt the magnitude of the lie she'd just told roll across her like a steamroller. Her mother's friend, who only moments before had seemed so real, now vanished. "It was a surprise," she managed to say weakly, but Annie was looking at her with suspicion. "I'm sorry I lied before," she added, apologizing for a lie that had really been the truth. She lowered her eyes and silently willed Annie to go outside. She could never undo this one.

"Don't you want to go to the library yourself, Charlotte?" Miss Brown asked her as Annie went off that afternoon with two books.

"No, thank you," Charlotte said without looking up. "Not right now." She heard Miss Brown sigh and felt her eyes staring at the top of her head. Charlotte studied her paper intently. Eventually, Miss Brown turned away.

"Sooner or later you'll have to go to the library," Annie predicted on the way home. "Miss Brown'll make you."

Charlotte shook her head. "She can't make me. It's a free country."

Annie laughed. "Not at school it isn't," she began. But as usual, Charlotte had stopped listening. She was gesturing wildly for silence. Annie sighed and stopped.

"What?" she whispered finally when she could not discover any reason for standing in silence.

Charlotte's eyes widened. She pointed at the bushes. Annie saw a small gray cat staring out at them.

"Oh!" she cried in excitement. "How cute!" She started toward the bushes, but the cat fled.

"You imbecile!" Charlotte shrieked in her ear. "You spoiled everything!"

Annie backed off, bewildered. Charlotte was sorry for her outburst. "You can't pet that cat," she said more gently. She peered after it, but it was nowhere in sight. "It's a wild cat."

Annie looked at her in disbelief. Her eyes narrowed. "There aren't any wild cats around here," she said. "That was just a regular cat."

"But it's a *wild* regular cat," Charlotte explained as they walked. "It's not used to people. It has to be tamed, a little bit at a time. I'm taming it. That's *my* cat."

Annie laughed. "That isn't your cat," she said. "That's probably the Pascals' cat. It's in their yard."

"And they hate it. They have wild cats all over the place, and if they catch them they take them to the shelter and they get put to sleep. Forever." Charlotte shook her head, sadly.

"What?" Annie stopped walking and stared at her again in disbelief. "They don't kill cats at the shelter. They shelter them. That's why they call it a *shelter*."

"Oh, sure. For *five days* they shelter them. Then, if nobody's adopted them, it's good-bye, cats. They'd have a million cats by now if they didn't kill them. That's how my mom learned about the insides of animals—cutting open cats from the animal shelter. They give them away free after they're dead."

Annie gasped in alarm. "But what if the Pascals catch that little gray cat?" she asked. "Could you get it from the shelter and adopt it?"

Charlotte shook her head. "My mom would never go for that. She says a pet in our house would be neglected because she works. She'd never adopt a pet on purpose. Only by accident."

They were in front of her house. Charlotte lowered her voice. "We've had injured birds and squirrels and everything at our house. My mom can't say no once an animal is here, I *know* she can't." Her voice faltered at the thought that she might very well be wrong about this. After all, her mother was a person who could cut open dead cats. "And I'll just tell her, *I'll* take care of it. It won't be neglected. Anyway, it already *is* neglected. Living in an empty house is better than being dead." She shuddered, thinking about her gray cat. Annie was staring at her in concern.

"You forgot to go home," Charlotte said to her, but Annie didn't move. She had begun to frown.

"What a trick to play on cats!" The frown became a scowl. "Calling it a *shelter*. It isn't fair." She pushed up her glasses and lifted her chin.

Charlotte agreed. "But *life* isn't fair," she announced. This was what her father replied whenever *she* complained. She wanted to see if it had the same effect on Annie it always had on her. It did. Annie looked furious.

"When *I* grow up," she said, clutching her books to her chest and turning to go, "*I'm* going to change things!" And off she marched.

6

Charlotte dumped the contents of her book bag onto her bedspread and stared at the stickers. She wondered if by any miracle her mother might really know a sticker-factory owner. Or maybe she could meet somebody, fast. If Charlotte showed a real interest in stickers, her mother might go out of her way to meet a factory owner.

"Aren't these interesting?" she said that night to her mother, who was leaning across her desk, studying sheets of papers that were spread everywhere. Her mother looked up blankly and glanced at the stickers.

"Hm," she said. She went back to work.

"I'm going to collect them," Charlotte said. "I'm trying to get the best sticker collection in the class. Maybe the world."

Her mother smiled and rubbed her forehead.

"I'm sure you will," she said absently.

"What I need," Charlotte continued, her hopes sinking, "is somebody who can get me stickers nobody else has. Like a factory owner or something. You know?"

Her mother looked up, finally turning her attention to the stickers Charlotte held in front of her. "You're really interested," she said.

Charlotte nodded earnestly. "Smell these," she insisted. Her mother laughed loudly at the old shoes.

"But everybody has them," Charlotte pointed out. "I want some that are different. I want to go to New York. To a factory."

Her mother smiled and went back to studying the papers on her desk. "Collecting doesn't work that way," she said. "You have to build a collection a little bit at a time, as things turn up. It's more fun that way."

She would have to quit school, Charlotte thought. Ten more days in the fifth grade and then she'd have to quit.

"I think you made all that up about the sticker factory," Tina said accusingly. She was standing over Charlotte while she did her spelling. Charlotte looked up. Laura and Jenny stood behind her, looking uneasy.

"Well then, don't come," Charlotte said, bend-

45

ing across her work. She sensed Laura and Jenny were on her side. "The car's going to be too full, anyway."

Tina was silent. Charlotte watched the blue and gray Nikes planted firmly beside her desk.

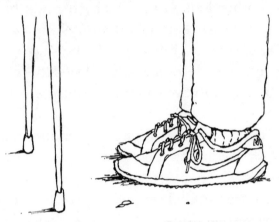

They didn't move. She changed "lickwid" to "liq-uid" and turned to the next page. Bent over, she felt like someone about to get her head chopped off. Her neck began to tingle. Laura and Jenny hadn't said a word in her defense.

"You better be telling the truth," Tina said. "That's all I got to say."

But after that, Laura and Jenny were nicer to her. They asked her where she lived and where she'd gotten her looseleaf notebook with the cat picture on it. Laura even gave her two stickers for free.

Charlotte tried to push the memory of her promise to the back of her mind. The trip was nine days away. Millions of things could happen between now and then. Besides, by that time, the girls might even like her so much they wouldn't care about her lie.

"You're going to start playing with them instead of me," Annie said unhappily on the way home.

Charlotte was surprised. "Why do you think that?" she said. "You're my best friend." But there were movie stars who ignored their old friends once they were famous. Some people were like that. Was she?

"I don't feel like your best friend anymore," Annie said. "You never want to do things with me."

"Well, after school I have to see Pippi," Charlotte pointed out. "And you can't play on weekends."

"Weekends I have to see my dad." Annie looked at her strangely, as if there were something Charlotte should reply to this. Charlotte couldn't think what to say. She knew about Annie's weekends with her dad. They'd been going on for months, ever since the divorce. Her father took her to neat places. "*Every* weekend," Annie added. "Even

47

the weekend of the factory trip."

"Oh!" Charlotte cleared her throat. "Well, that's too bad," she said. "I really wanted you to come. You most of all."

Beside her, Annie looked glum. Charlotte wished she would stop dragging her feet. Hadn't she said what Annie wanted to hear? And meant it, too. If there *were* a trip, Charlotte would want *her*, most of all, to come on it.

"Well, how about now?" Annie demanded. "I could come with you while you feed Pippi."

Charlotte shook her head. "It would scare her," she said. "She's only used to me." She wanted Annie to go home. She was tired of feeling guilty all the time.

Obligingly, Annie wandered off without a word. Charlotte watched her go.

But, carrying Pippi's milk carefully through neighboring backyards to the Pascals', Charlotte kept seeing Annie's unhappy face. Was it true she was going to stop playing with her? She *was* busy lately. And Annie had begun to seem like a stray cat herself. The kind that followed you home and sat meowing on your step, driving you nuts.

She should have let her come along to feed Pippi, Charlotte thought remorsefully. It wouldn't have mattered if she stood across the street and watched. The truth was, she didn't want to share her cat with anyone.

And Pippi rewarded her loyalty. For the first time, she was waiting for Charlotte when she arrived. She emerged from the bushes before Charlotte even set down the bowl of milk. Charlotte's heart thumped loudly in excitement. She set the bowl down carefully, close to the cat, and didn't back away.

"It's okay," Charlotte whispered. "It's just me." She wondered if the loud beating of her heart would frighten Pippi. "Come on," she said gently, and to her amazement, Pippi came. Charlotte tried not to move while she lapped the milk. "Shut up," she willed the thumping in her chest.

When she'd finished the milk, Pippi cleaned her face and paws and sat still, not quite looking at Charlotte but not quite looking away, either. "Rub against me," Charlotte begged silently, and the cat seemed to consider it. She began to pace. "Come on," Charlotte said, but this time her words sent Pippi into the bushes.

"It's all right," Charlotte said aloud to the bushes. "I'll give you another chance."

"Who are you talking to?"

Charlotte turned, startled, to see her sister Ruth on her way home from band practice at the junior high. Ruth played the clarinet, but Charlotte always thought of her as the tuba whenever she heard the band play.

"Nobody." She started walking so that her sister wouldn't spot the empty bowl on the grass.

"Nobody?" Ruth said, following. "Now you talk to bushes? Do you tell lies to bushes?" She giggled.

"Stop it!" Charlotte said angrily, but her sister continued to walk behind her, snickering.

"You're going to be sorry you're so mean!" Charlotte burst out in sudden rage, spinning around. "Pippi's going to hate your guts and you'll be sorry you're such a jerk."

Her sister looked surprised. "Pippi?" she asked.

"Yes, Pippi!" But Charlotte felt the defiance drain out of her at the realization of what she'd said. Tears sprang from her eyes against her will. "She's mine, and I'll kill you if you ever even touch her," she said weakly, wiping at her face with her sleeve. Ruth was studying her in alarm. She wore the expression their mother wore when she was about to place her hand on Charlotte's forehead and see if she had a fever.

"Don't you touch me!" Charlotte screamed, her anger returning. Ruth backed off. Charlotte stormed toward the house with giant strides, leaving Ruth bewildered on the sidewalk.

50

By dinnertime, Charlotte was alarmed by the things she'd said to her sister. She waited to hear how Ruth would present them at the dinner table, but her sister was silent. Occasionally she looked at Charlotte and away again, as if she were contagious and even the slightest eye contact could cause her germs to spread. Charlotte was, in fact, beginning to feel ill. Her stomach flopped up and down every time she tried to swallow anything.

"You aren't eating, Charlotte," her mother said. "Are you sick?" She came around the table to place her hand on Charlotte's forehead. Charlotte shook her head and pulled herself loose. If her mother thought she was sick, she'd send her to bed for the weekend. If she didn't go to see Pippi tomorrow, the cat might forget her, or starve to death.

"I feel fine," Charlotte said, taking a huge bite of mashed potatoes. They felt like mush in her mouth. Slowly, methodically, she chewed and swallowed.

Her mother sighed. Charlotte wondered why she always made people sigh. She took another bite and swallowed.

"You worry me to death, Charlotte," her mother said, sitting down again at the table. "There is always something going on in that mind of yours that we don't know about."

Charlotte looked at her sisters and father smiling at her mother's remark. Wasn't there something going on in everyone's mind all the time? It sounded, to her, like a dumb thing to say, but she didn't comment.

7

On Saturday morning the telephone rang. Charlotte always answered expectantly, though calls were seldom for her. Inside every telephone lurked possible surprise.

"Charlotte?"

The voice was vaguely familiar. Charlotte felt a tingle of apprehension. "Yes?"

"You're lying," the voice said. Tina's voice.

Charlotte's palms began to sweat. "Who is this?" she demanded with a show of bravado.

There was a grunt on the other end of the line. "You know who it is," Tina said. "I don't believe in your sticker factory. I want proof."

"Proof?" Charlotte leaned out the kitchen doorway, listening to make certain her mother was still cleaning upstairs. She heard the reassuring sound of the vacuum cleaner in the distance. No one else was home. "I'm going to take you there, for Pete's sake," she said loudly, moving back into the safety of the kitchen. "Isn't that proof enough?"

"Let me talk to your mother," Tina demanded.

Her mother? The tingle of apprehension raced down Charlotte's spine again. "She isn't here," she lied. "My mother's a very busy woman. You can't bother her."

There was silence while Tina considered her next maneuver. Charlotte counted flowers in the wallpaper and prayed her mother would not decide to use the upstairs phone.

"Think of some other proof then," Tina demanded. "By Monday." Charlotte heard a click and the line was dead.

Proof? Even if there were a sticker factory, Charlotte didn't know how she could prove it. "It's not fair," she said to the humming receiver. Tina was never fair.

She spent the next five minutes staring at the phone, her mind a blank, trying desperately to think of proof. Not one thought entered her head.

"This is what it's like to be my sisters," she told herself in a burst of amazement. They *never* had thoughts. None that counted, anyway.

The kitchen suddenly seemed big and unfriendly. There were so many chairs without people sitting in them. Charlotte wandered through the dining room and the living room, trying to feel safe and loved in her own home. She felt totally alone. Whatever Tina did to her when she found out the truth would probably be what she deserved, and not one person in this house or anywhere else on earth would stick up for her.

Annie would have once, Charlotte thought sadly, leaning her elbows on the windowsill and staring out into the deserted street—where was everyone? Even the sound of her mother's vacuum had stopped. Now Annie must hate her. She'd said she was weird. And Charlotte had lied to her. She blinked hard to hold back tears. This is Loneliness, she thought. This is the way people felt when they jumped off bridges. Or became bag ladies. Bag ladies were just weird, lonely children who grew up. The thought thrilled her with its awfulness. No *wonder* Annie hated being an only child in an empty house!

Then she remembered Pippi, who was like a little bag cat. Charlotte hadn't even fed her today! Ashamed, she rushed to the kitchen to search the cupboards for the biggest bowl they owned. Pippi was too skinny. What if this milk were the only thing the poor cat had to eat? What if she didn't like birds and mice? Her very life depended on

Charlotte! How could she waste time being lonely?

Charlotte pulled out the blue ceramic serving dish her mother used when they had company. It was, in Charlotte's opinion, the most beautiful thing they owned. Little yellow flowers were painted around the edge of the inside. Charlotte stared at it. No one would have to know if she just borrowed this dish. Her father had taken her sisters to ballet lessons. She could have it home and put away by the time anyone even came into the kitchen.

"I'll be very, very careful," Charlotte promised her mother in a whisper as she filled the bowl with milk. Her mother was now vacuuming in the front bedrooms. Charlotte hurried. It was a perfect time to escape out the back. But she had difficulty managing the back door with her hands wrapped around the bowl. Drops of milk plopped onto the floor and steps. If she left a trail of milk from here to the Pascals', would Pippi follow them home? She did leave drops all the way. She'd filled the bowl too full. Still, there was plenty of milk left by the time she arrived at the bushes.

Again Pippi seemed to have been waiting. Charlotte thought that if the cat were a dog she'd be wagging her tail. She sniffed at the new dish curiously before she drank.

"Pretty, isn't it?" Charlotte asked softly. Pippi

began to drink. "If you come to live at my house, you'll have bowls as pretty as that every day of your life." The cat lapped furiously in excitement. Charlotte sat on the ground and watched, pulling her knees up close to her chest. Leaves were falling from the trees.

"It's going to be winter soon," she whispered. "We have heat at my house." Pippi looked at her, milk dripping from her chin. Charlotte dared to reach out and touch the cat on the head, very gently. Pippi drew back but she didn't run away. Charlotte left her hand out, and the cat sniffed at it.

"This is the hand of the person who feeds you," Charlotte said unnecessarily. Pippi sat down and looked at her. Charlotte thought she should say something especially convincing.

"I'm a cat lover," she said. Pippi didn't move. "I'm a lover of gray cats. Gray is my favorite color." Pippi began washing her face. Charlotte thought she looked satisfied.

"I have to take this bowl home now," she said, finally, emptying the remaining milk into the pink bowl that was still sitting there from yesterday. "My mom would kill me if she knew I let a cat drink out of this dish. Not that she doesn't like cats," she hastened to add. "She just *loves* this dish. She wouldn't even let *me* drink out of it."

Pippi moved back to the edge of the bushes and lay down, obviously content. Charlotte felt a glow of excitement. Pippi was used to her. "You are *my* cat," Charlotte said as she left her there.

Charlotte's mother was in the kitchen when she returned. Charlotte stood outside the back door, clutching the bowl in terror. Her mother, looking up from the sink, saw Charlotte's face framed in the glass. She scowled and gestured for Charlotte to come inside. Hastily, Charlotte set the dish behind the shrub next to the door.

"Where have you been?" Mrs. Cheetham demanded crossly.

Charlotte shrugged. "Nowhere," she said, though she knew that, to a scientist, "nowhere" was not a satisfactory answer.

"I wanted to take you shopping for new jeans." Mrs. Cheetham looked disapprovingly at the ones Charlotte had on. There were holes in both knees. "Now there won't be time. You should tell me before you take off, Charlotte."

"Sorry," Charlotte said. In truth, she felt a swell of relief that she'd escaped before her mother had dragged her off to a store.

"You sit right there at that table," her mother directed. "We're going to eat as soon as your sisters come in the door."

Charlotte sat. She thought of her sisters coming

in the door. There was no way her sisters would make it past the bushes without seeing the bowl. Charlotte began to sweat. Her turtleneck jersey was suddenly very hot and scratchy.

"What was this doing in the bushes?" Mr. Cheetham asked when he finally returned with Ruth and Marie. He came into the kitchen carrying the ceramic dish. Charlotte felt little rivers of sweat running down her chest inside the jersey.

"The bushes?" Mrs. Cheetham grabbed the bowl and examined it for damage. "My best dish in the bushes?" She looked up quizzically and studied each of the girls' faces. When she saw Charlotte, she knew.

"What was this doing outside, Charlotte?" she demanded.

Eight eyes were glaring at her. Charlotte swallowed hard. "I don't know," she said meekly, but she knew "I don't know" answers were no more acceptable than "nowhere" ones.

"This is a handmade bowl, Charlotte. One of a kind. My favorite. You know all those things, don't you?" Charlotte nodded. "Then you tell me what you were doing with it outside the house."

Charlotte looked down at the table. She thought she could think better if everyone didn't stare at her.

"Explain, Charlotte."

"I was feeding a cat," she answered finally, surprised to hear herself telling the truth.

"Feeding a cat? With my best bowl?" Her mother looked incredulous. "What cat?"

"The one in our backyard," Charlotte said eagerly. "The one who's dying of starvation. The one who's probably wounded, too." Her voice faltered at this last embellishment, but she saw that her mother's face had softened a bit. "I thought the bowl would cheer her up."

"I haven't seen any cats in our yard," Mrs. Cheetham said. She looked at the others for confirmation. Their faces were blank.

Charlotte nodded. "Well, sometimes in our yard," she said. "Sometimes at the Pascals'. But she likes it here best. She *loves* it here."

60

Everyone was quiet while they considered this information. Ruth looked at her with narrowed eyes.

"It must be one of the cats born under the Pascals' porch," her father said suddenly. "A couple of months ago. She was talking about poisoning them."

Charlotte's eyes widened. She thought of Pippi drinking out of a bowl of poison. Panic rose in her chest.

"What do you mean it's wounded?" her mother asked seriously.

Charlotte wished that Pippi had at least a little limp. The kind that didn't hurt. "Well, sometimes she seems to limp. And she's really skinny. You can see bones poking out. I couldn't just let her *die*," she said dramatically. She could see she was having the desired effect. Her mother looked worried.

"Charlotte, we can't be feeding an animal like that. It isn't fair to the cat. She'll think we're going to take care of her and we really aren't."

"Yes, we are!" Charlotte insisted. "*I* take care of her. I give her milk every day."

Her mother shook her head in exasperation. "That isn't a proper diet," she said. "You can't just feed a cat now and then and come indoors. It's cruel."

"I'm just warming her up," Charlotte said. "Getting her used to me so she can live with us."

"But she's wild," Mr. Cheetham protested.

Charlotte shook her head anxiously. "Not anymore," she said. "She comes right up to me. She's crazy about me, I can tell. She just wouldn't be happy with anyone else."

Mrs. Cheetham's face relaxed into what seemed to be the beginning of a smile. She looked again at her husband. "The next time you feed this cat," she said to Charlotte, "I want to get a look at her."

8

"I have to bring my mother tomorrow," Charlotte explained to Pippi that afternoon. "Limp a little," she suggested. She saw, happily, that Pippi had finished the milk in the pink bowl. Still, her mother had said that milk wasn't a proper diet. She looked at Pippi worriedly. She was about to reach out and attempt to pet the cat when a voice startled her.

"Charlotte, are you the one who's been feeding that animal?" Charlotte stood up to face Mrs. Pascal. She couldn't decide what to say.

"Feeding her?" she said finally.

"Don't play dumb," Mrs. Pascal said. She kicked out in the direction of the cat, who had headed for cover in the bushes and was now peering out from beneath a thick, low branch. "Shoo!" Mrs.

Pascal said. Pippi disappeared. "I don't want any cats around here. I don't want them getting fed on my property. You want this one, you take it home. You hear me?"

Charlotte nodded. She reached down for the pink bowl. "I'm going to do that," she said earnestly. "My mother's coming over here tomorrow to look at her and just be sure she's the one we want. Then we'll take her home."

Mrs. Pascal looked skeptical. "No more feeding her then. You understand?"

Charlotte nodded again. She looked at the bushes, trying to discern a small gray face, hoping that Pippi was hearing and understanding just how important all this was.

"Mrs. Pascal won't let me feed her," Charlotte sobbed that night to her mother when she was getting into bed. She hadn't planned to tell her mother about her afternoon visit to Pippi, but fear ate away at her resolution.

"What?" Mrs. Cheetham asked, concerned.

"She'll starve to death," Charlotte cried when she'd explained. "She's used to my bringing her a bowl of milk every day. She'll be so hungry she'll eat a bowl of poison."

Mrs. Cheetham looked thoughtful. She rubbed Charlotte's back, trying to calm her. "We'll think of something," she promised. "Don't worry."

But how could she not worry? Charlotte thought, lying awake and staring into the darkness. She tried to identify reassuring shapes that loomed around her bed—her bookcase, her desk, her various stuffed animals—but nothing comforted her. She kept imagining Pippi drinking from a bowl of poison.

And Tina. In the background of every picture that popped into her mind, there was Tina, looking angry and mean. Tina wanted proof. What kind of proof? Charlotte couldn't think of anything. She tossed anxiously and threw her pillow onto the floor. She would never sleep. Never.

But she did. She drifted in and out, hearing voices, seeing faces, picturing Pippi dead. "You're weird," Annie called to Charlotte across a street. Charlotte sat upright in bed, suddenly sure that Annie knew. She knew what a rotten best friend she had. Charlotte had lied to her, as if she were Tina or Laura and not someone she could trust. *Annie* would never demand proof. Proof! There was Tina again, looking fierce and bossy.

Charlotte put her feet over the edge of the bed and turned on her bedside light. What would be proof? she thought for the hundredth time. A note from her mother saying she knew a factory owner? Charlotte tried to think of someone who wrote like a grown-up who might do such a thing for her. No one came to mind. She didn't know any forgers.

Or just a letter maybe, from someone in New York. Charlotte could say it was from the factory owner. After all, the person wouldn't write "I am a factory owner" in a letter to her friends. Any letter would do.

Who did her mother know in New York? She had friends there who were scientists, but Charlotte didn't know their names. She sighed. Somewhere in this house there must be a letter from someone in New York. She would borrow it. But where would it be? Rummaging in her mind for all the places letters would be stored, Charlotte suddenly remembered. Margaret! Her mother's cousin Margaret lived in New York. She'd come to visit them in the summer and written a post-card afterwards to thank them. Charlotte had that postcard somewhere. It had a picture of the Statue of Liberty on the front. Her mother had wanted her to save it.

Charlotte hurried across the room to her desk. She opened drawers and began searching through piles of old papers. For once she wished she were neat. Why did she save all this old junk? Still, if she didn't save old junk, she wouldn't have this postcard that was buried here somewhere, would she? The postcard that was about to save her life.

She found it on the bottom of the third drawer—the Statue of Liberty on the front of a postcard that read, "I enjoyed my visit so much. Why don't you all come up here? I'd love to show you around. Love, Margaret." Perfect. It was perfect. Or as perfect as it could be without mentioning a sticker factory. And there was the New York postmark, too. Unfortunately, there was also a date, as clear as day. Charlotte wanted this to be the postcard that had just arrived, after the factory owner's visit last week. The date, however, was very clearly June 1985 Charlotte needed it to be October.

After searching her drawers again for her stamp pad, Charlotte set to work smudging the dated part of the postmark. It wasn't really smudged—just covered up. If Tina tried, she could probably unsmudge it and discover the truth. Charlotte sighed. It was the best she could do.

She slipped back into bed and turned out the light, the postcard hidden safely beneath the blotter of her desk. Exhausted, she slept.

"If we could just make her come into our yard," Charlotte said the next day on the way to the Pascals'. "If she'd just come once, I know she'd want to stay there."

68

Mrs. Cheetham stopped walking and looked at Charlotte. "You told me you'd seen her in our yard lots of times."

Charlotte hung her head.

"Did you also make up the part about Mrs. Pascal telling you to take this cat home?" her mother demanded.

"No!" But it was the sort of thing she *would* have made up if it hadn't really happened. Why should her mother believe her? "It's true," she said desperately. "You can even ask Mrs. Pascal."

Mrs. Cheetham frowned and continued walking. She was annoyed now. Charlotte was afraid her annoyance would spill over onto Pippi and she wouldn't want to bring her home.

"I'm going to try to stop lying," Charlotte promised sincerely. "I'm going to try every day." Her mother was silent. "Maybe it's stuck in me though," Charlotte said morosely. "The lying part. I mean I say lies when I don't really mean to."

Her mother sighed loudly. "I guess it *is* an instinct of sorts," she said, sounding tired. "Sort of like the one animals have for self-preservation."

Charlotte wasn't sure she understood this, but it seemed to make her mother less unhappy, so she nodded.

"It doesn't mean it's right," her mother hastened to add. "But I guess you won't feel the need to lie when you get older and have more power over things."

Pippi was sitting on the grass in front of the bushes. She began to pace when Charlotte and her mother approached.

"See," Charlotte said. "She's waiting for her milk! She'll hate me for not bringing it."

"And that," said Mrs. Cheetham, "is why you shouldn't feed animals that don't belong to you." But her voice wasn't stern. She bent down and rubbed her hand along Pippi's back. Charlotte watched in amazement.

"She's really still a kitten," Mrs. Cheetham said thoughtfully. "And I'd say you're right—she's not wild anymore."

"Maybe we could get a box," Charlotte suggested eagerly. "We could carry her back to our yard."

Mrs. Cheetham seemed to consider it. "I think a box would frighten her," she said finally. "And I don't know that she'd stay in our yard. She'd probably come back here where things are familiar to her." Pippi had moved off and was sniffing the grass in obvious search for her milk. Mrs. Cheetham caught the cat unawares from behind and swept her from the ground.

Charlotte was left standing there, startled. She watched her mother move off down the side-walk, accompanied by the sound of tiny meows. She hurried to catch up. When she was closer she caught a glimpse of Pippi's face, hanging terrified over the edge of Mrs. Cheetham's arm. Her ears lay back against her head as if she'd been sat on.

"Mom!" Charlotte said, frightened, either for herself or for Pippi, she didn't know which. Things were moving too swiftly. But Mrs. Cheetham wouldn't slow down.

"Good kitty," she was saying as Pippi struggled to wriggle off under her armpit. Mrs. Cheetham pulled her up, and the face appeared over her sleeve again. Charlotte giggled, in spite of herself. She felt a thrill of excitement.

"Good kitty," her mother said again. Charlotte watched her in appreciation. She was cooing at the cat the way she often cooed at babies. Acting as if things were just fine, while she was moving down the street at a near run.

"I can promise you this is a good cat," Charlotte said earnestly.

Mrs. Cheetham nodded and turned to smile at her daughter without losing step.

9

Pippi was frightened at being indoors. Mrs. Cheetham ordered everyone to stay away from her.

"That's easy enough to do," Marie said. Pippi had long since disappeared into a closet. Charlotte didn't think it was easy at all. She was desperate for Pippi to love her. In one week there might be no one else who did.

Mr. Cheetham was sent to the store for litter and cat food. "Don't get bird flavors," Charlotte instructed. "I don't think she likes those." She was annoyed when everyone laughed. "It's true," she insisted. "I know this cat better than anyone. It's *my* cat." She looked around in defiance.

Only Ruth looked back. "Then how come she won't let you pet her?" She smirked. Charlotte went speechless with rage. She hated Ruth! *Hated* her!

"Well, she's frightened," Mrs. Cheetham replied calmly, as if this should be obvious to everyone, even Ruth. It *was* obvious. Charlotte just hadn't thought to say it. "Eventually she'll let all of us pet her."

Charlotte doubted it. She couldn't imagine anyone ever growing to like being touched by one of her sisters. The cat was going to love only *her*.

"You are *my* cat now," she whispered to Pippi when she finally emerged from the closet. Charlotte followed her from room to room at a safe distance. "It's a good idea to be nice to my mother, but you're really mine." In the kitchen she tried once to pet her, but Pippi peed on the floor in fright. Charlotte cleaned it up with a napkin before her mother could see, grateful that it had happened here and not on the rug.

In the living room, Pippi ran behind the sofa and refused to come out. Charlotte watched from the other side of the room so that she could see both ends. She could hear Pippi's claws picking at the back of the sofa. Her mother would have a fit! But if Charlotte yelled and scared her, Pippi might pee again. Which was worse, Charlotte wondered—a shredded sofa or a smelly rug? A smelly rug, she decided. Her mother would notice that. She might not find the shreds on the back of the sofa for years.

She wondered how long it would take for Pippi to become a member of the family, so that no matter what she did no one could throw her out. That was one thing you could be certain of in a family. People might get mad at you, but they had to keep right on letting you live with them. It was why her sisters were still alive, she thought. Her mother and father *had* to take care of them, no matter how disgusting they were. It occurred to her that this would apply to her own upcoming disgrace. At least she'd have a place to live.

Pippi darted suddenly from behind the sofa into the kitchen. Charlotte followed, keeping her distance. Pippi had leaped onto the counter and skidded to a halt, finding no place to hide.

"You'd better get down from there," Charlotte whispered, alarmed. Pippi was walking the counter, sniffing everything. "Get down!" Charlotte commanded. She was afraid to lift her. Pippi looked at her and began chewing the cord to the telephone.

"Oh good grief," Charlotte said under her breath. She swung the end of the cord so that it slapped gently against the cat's face. Pippi let go and jumped onto the floor. She looked up at

Charlotte before walking off. "You don't live here yet," Charlotte explained gently. "You have to be good for at least a day." Pippi didn't seem convinced. She strolled off again into the dining room, where she encountered Mrs. Cheetham.

"What a good little cat," Charlotte heard her mother saying. "Aren't you being a good little thing?" In the kitchen, Charlotte rolled her eyes and smiled.

"Maybe I could manage it," Annie said on Monday morning as they neared school. They were the first words she'd said that Charlotte heard. She'd been thinking of the postcard buried deep in her book bag and of Tina's threatening voice on the telephone.

"What?" Charlotte said, vaguely eyeing her friend. "Manage what?"

"To come on the trip." Annie looked directly into Charlotte's eyes. "Maybe I could explain to my father. After all, a trip to a sticker factory is a really big deal, and you're my best friend. He'd understand."

Charlotte swallowed hard and looked away. She felt Annie's eyes boring holes in the side of her face. She *did* know! She knew and she wanted Charlotte to tell her the truth, the way a real friend would. Charlotte swallowed again. Her book bag felt strangely weightless, as if everything, even the postcard, had slipped out the bottom and disappeared. Charlotte clutched it to her chest and tried to say the words: *It was all a lie. A big, fat lie.* Annie would understand. She was waiting. But somehow, Charlotte couldn't do it. Annie's knowing just made it worse.

"Well?" Tina said. Charlotte was bent over her desk, trying to look busy. She had the postcard, but somehow the closer she got to Tina, the less likely it seemed that Tina would fall for it.

"Here." Charlotte reached into her desk and handed the card nonchalantly to Tina. She pretended to be engrossed in the book she was reading.

"So what's this supposed to be?" Tina demanded. "It's just a postcard."

Charlotte looked up, annoyed. "It's from my mother's friend," she said impatiently. "It thanks us for letting her visit. This is the card that made my mother decide we had to see the dumb sticker place."

"It doesn't say anything on here about a sticker factory," Tina said, dropping it back onto Charlotte's desk. "What kind of proof is this?"

"Perfectly good proof," Charlotte said, tucking the card inside the book she was reading and trying to look engrossed again. "If you don't believe this," she said to Tina without looking up, "you won't believe anything."

With all the confusion, Charlotte had forgotten that Monday was her day to give the Current Events speech. Miss Brown would be furious, Charlotte thought anxiously when she remembered. If she kept this up, she would flunk out of school. Charlotte sat upright, amazed. Here was a new idea! Why hadn't she thought of it before? If she flunked everything, Miss Brown would suggest sending her to a private school, where she'd have more supervision. That had happened to Larry Neigle. What had really happened was that the teacher couldn't stand the sight of him anymore. Charlotte thought Miss Brown might feel that way about her very soon. Maybe within the week. She'd never see Tina again.

"Charlotte?" Miss Brown said at ten o'clock. "Current Events, please."

Charlotte walked to the front of the room. She had planned to simply announce that she hadn't done the assignment and receive an F, but with everyone staring at her, flunking suddenly seemed too embarrassing.

Once in front of the room, however, she

realized she had nothing to say. Miss Brown sat at her desk, waiting.

"Yes, Charlotte?" she said.

Charlotte took a deep breath. "My Current Events topic is wild cats," she began. This caused a mild stir of amusement to ripple through the classroom and settle into expectancy. Charlotte blossomed in the face of this receptive audience. She smiled. Her wild beast grew a bit. It growled and scratched ferociously.

"Charlotte," Miss Brown interrupted impatiently. "Current Events refers to something important that's happening in the world at this particular time. I think you know that."

Charlotte nodded and cleared her throat. "This particular current event is happening at my house," she began. Miss Brown's expression darkened, but Charlotte didn't care. She was imagining myriad ways to describe the capture of the wild beast. Pippi was a ball of vicious gray fur.

"It has to do with a cat I've had to tame. A *completely* wild animal."

This time the laughter was raucous and mocking, and Miss Brown looked decidedly unhappy. Charlotte realized they thought she was lying. Already! All she'd said was the truth. Her ears began to turn red. It was hard to look like you

were telling the truth if everyone expected you
to lie.

"It's true," she insisted, shouting above the
squawks and wisecracks. "It wasn't the jungle
kind of wild cat," she amended stubbornly. "It
was just a cat nobody'd ever petted." The class
was quiet again. "And the world's probably full
of wild cats," Charlotte added for Miss Brown's
benefit. "My mother and I tamed this one, so it
can be done." Stories of capture and defeat tum-
bled through her head again, but she wisely ignored them.

"What's its name?" Jeffrey interrupted to ask.

Charlotte squirmed uneasily, deflated. She
looked at Miss Brown and then down at the floor.
"Pippi," she said weakly, wondering if Miss Brown

79

would think she was being defiant. Again everyone laughed. "It just acts like a Pippi," Charlotte said angrily. "I can't help that. It's just sort of the name the cat *came* with." But of course, wild cats didn't come with names.

"All right, Charlotte," Miss Brown said in exasperation. "It's lovely you have a cat named Pippi. It does, however, have very little to do with Current Events. Please go home tonight and read the newspaper. This report has earned you an F."

Charlotte nodded and made her way back to her seat, followed, she was certain, by the silent laughter of twenty-two of her classmates. She suspected they didn't even believe she had a cat. She sighed and fell into her seat. Well, at least she had gotten her F. That was something.

Later in the day, Miss Brown called her up to her desk. To Charlotte's amazement, the teacher looked friendly. There was no sign of the Lecture Look.

"Charlotte, I've decided I made a mistake. I think you should be able to check whatever you'd like out of the library." Miss Brown smiled expectantly, waiting for Charlotte's look of pleasure. Charlotte tried to muster one but couldn't.

"Okay," she said. "Thank you."

"Would you like to go to the library this afternoon?" her teacher asked.

Charlotte shook her head. Her ears began to hurt just thinking of Mrs. Arnold. In all the recent excitement, she'd almost forgotten her problems with the librarian. Miss Brown looked confused.

"I mean, it's just—" Charlotte was trying to think of an explanation that wasn't exactly a lie. "I have all the Pippi books at home now," she said in defeat. She wondered if her mother would call this lie self-preservation.

Miss Brown sighed and nodded, and Charlotte knew that for the moment she had said all she was going to say about the library. But Charlotte felt guilty for lying so soon after her promise to her mother. Her feet wouldn't carry her back to her desk.

"I guess that was a lie," she said softly. She tried to look Miss Brown in the eye, but stared, instead, at her small round chin. She watched Miss Brown's mouth drop open in surprise.

"I just don't want to go to the library right now," she explained. She dared a peek at her teacher's eyes and saw that they did not look angry. "I don't have much time for reading right now with my new cat and all." Was *that* a lie? Charlotte considered and decided that it wasn't. Not exactly.

"All right, Charlotte," Miss Brown said. "Thank

81

you for explaining. And for telling me the truth."

Charlotte nodded in relief and went back to her desk.

"A wild cat," Tina said at lunch, rolling her eyes.

Charlotte glared at her. "I said a *regular* wild cat. It just wasn't tamed yet."

"Right." Tina looked around the table, assessing her audience. Everyone was listening. "Didn't you use to have an anteater a few years ago, too?" she asked triumphantly, eliciting gleeful chuckles from all corners of the table.

Charlotte flushed. She didn't think anyone remembered her anteater story.

"This is true," Annie said, coming to her defense. "I've seen Pippi."

"Oh, I believe you," Tina said sarcastically. "Just like I believe the story about the sticker factory. Maybe I'll get a look at your wild cat when I come over to go to the factory." Her eyes were a challenge.

"Fine," Charlotte said, emboldened by the fact that Pippi did exist. "You might if you don't scare her to death." Once again she witnessed a wavering of Tina's confidence and felt it as a victory.

"Hey!" Tina said, suddenly sitting upright, her face brightening. "There's your sister."

Startled, Charlotte turned to look. Marie was always on safety duty during this lunch period. What was she doing in here? Reporting someone, Charlotte thought in disgust.

"I'm going to discuss this little trip with her," Tina said, swinging her leg over the bench and gesturing to Marie. Charlotte watched, stunned, as her sister smiled and crossed the cafeteria.

"Hello, kiddies," she said cheerfully.

"We were just discussing your new wild cat," Tina said, chuckling.

"Yeah?" Marie said. "So?"

Tina was only momentarily deflated. "And the sticker-factory owner," she added, significantly. Behind her, Charlotte opened her eyes wide and glared a silent desperate plea at her sister. I will do anything, she thought wildly, trying to say it with her eyes. I'll be your slave forever.

"*You* know," Charlotte managed to say weakly, "Margaret. In New York."

Marie's mouth twisted into a smirk. "Margaret?" she said, watching Charlotte's discomfort with obvious pleasure. "In New York?"

Tina turned abruptly to laugh in Charlotte's face, startling her. "It seems your sister has never heard of a sticker-factory owner in New York. Isn't that odd?"

"Oh, her," Marie said, her smirk broadening

into a grin. "You mean *Margaret*, in New York."

Tina's face fell. There was silence at the table. Charlotte closed her eyes in relief.

"What about her?" Marie continued.

Tina looked disgruntled. She swung her leg back over the bench and leaned across her lunch. "I just wondered," she said vaguely. "Are you coming on your mother's sticker-factory trip next weekend?"

Marie's expression changed from amusement to surprise. She looked at Charlotte, who looked away.

"I wouldn't dream of missing it," Marie said, continuing to stare at Charlotte, who continued to not stare back.

Charlotte and Annie sat silently side by side at the table and watched everyone else file out onto the playground. Charlotte's peanut-butter sandwich felt glued to the spot where her heart was supposed to be.

"Charlotte?" Annie said at last, quietly, not looking up. "Aren't you afraid?"

The peanut-butter sandwich seemed to thud, like a heart. Maybe she would have a heart attack, Charlotte thought hopefully.

"I mean Marie might tell your mother," Annie continued.

Charlotte couldn't believe her ears. She looked at Annie from the corner of her eye. Annie looked back, sheepish.

"I *thought* you knew," Charlotte whispered in shame, but relief was flooding through her. Annie's face was pinched with concern. "I'm going to get killed, aren't I?" Charlotte asked.

The look on Annie's face seemed to verify this. "Tina's going to kill you. Your mother's going to kill you. Everybody will kill you, Charlotte!" They sat a moment in silence, contemplating Charlotte's fate, but eventually, to Charlotte's disbelief, Annie began to smile. She sucked slowly on her straw, her eyes wide and cheerful above her milk carton.

"You're awful, Charlotte," she said, giggling, when she'd set down her milk. "I don't *believe* you!"

Charlotte nodded. Sometimes she didn't believe herself.

10

Charlotte ran home after school, hoping to arrive before her sisters. Pippi had been locked in the kitchen all day with her litter box and food dishes. Charlotte was terrified she'd destroyed something or gone to the bathroom on the floor. If she had, Charlotte wanted to clean up before anyone saw.

"Hi, Pippi!" she said more enthusiastically than she'd intended as she came through the back door. Her words startled the cat and sent her flying into the basement. "It's only me, your mother. Come on up here." But Pippi was not going to be talked into doing anything.

Charlotte began an inspection of the kitchen. Everything looked fine. Pippi had even used her litter box. The only sign of any foul play was the trash can lying on its side in the corner, but Charlotte knew that was acceptable cat fun. Her mother had said so. Pippi liked to bat wadded-up pieces of paper and tin foil around the floor.

"You are a good, good cat," Charlotte called down the stairs. Marie and Ruth came through the back door. "She was perfect," Charlotte said anxiously. "She didn't do one thing wrong." Her sisters looked around the kitchen suspiciously. Charlotte studiously avoided Marie's eyes.

"Good thing," Ruth said. She took a can of juice from the refrigerator and flipped off the lid.

The telephone rang. "Probably Mom," Ruth said. She leaned back against the counter and drank from the can, the way their father drank beer. "She wants to know how the cat behaved."

Charlotte glared at her and answered the telephone. "Hello?" she said, but there was no sound.

"Oh my God!" Ruth's expression was a mixture of amusement and amazement. She pointed at the cord dangling from the receiver as Charlotte pressed it to her ear. Charlotte looked down and saw that it was not attached to the telephone. It took her a moment to realize what had happened. Pippi had chewed completely through the cord!

"Pippi!" she gasped, hanging up the useless receiver and staring at the phone. She was afraid

87

to turn and face her sisters.

"You and that cat are going to get it," Ruth predicted in Charlotte's ear. As if to prove her right, the phone began to ring again.

"Run upstairs and answer," Ruth commanded, but Charlotte couldn't move. Marie tore willingly from the room and up the steps. She was going to tell on Pippi. Possibly on Charlotte and her sticker-factory lie.

"Did she sound mad?" Charlotte asked weakly when Marie came back down.

Marie shrugged. She smiled at Charlotte mysteriously.

"Well, what did she say?" Charlotte demanded, but Marie was not talking. Charlotte decided to be upstairs when her mother came home. At five-thirty she heard the car door slam. And then the kitchen door. Silence. Her mother didn't come looking for her. What did that mean? Charlotte's heart pounded in fear. Marie must be describing in detail everything Tina had said at lunch. Or they were punishing Pippi while she wasn't there to defend her! Charlotte opened the bedroom door and listened. The sounds coming up from the kitchen were normal dinner-preparation sounds.

"Charlotte?" her mother called, coming into the living room. Charlotte froze in her bedroom doorway. "Where are you?" She didn't sound angry. Charlotte came down the stairs cautiously. "Where've you been?" her mother asked.

Charlotte shrugged. "Upstairs." She looked at her mother's face suspiciously, seeing no trace of anger. Marie was saving the Tina story for the dinner table. But surely she'd told on Pippi. "Aren't you mad?" Charlotte said meekly.

Mrs. Cheetham laughed. "Why would I be mad?" she asked.

Charlotte's suspicions grew. Maybe her mother didn't know about Pippi either. Marie hadn't told her and she hadn't yet tried to use the phone. Charlotte didn't know what to say.

"You mean because of the telephone cord?" Mrs. Cheetham's eyes were still merry. Charlotte

89

stared at her in amazement. Her mother unbuttoned her white lab jacket and pulled it off. "Whew," she said, dropping it into a chair and sitting on top of it. "I am beat."

Charlotte watched and waited for the rest of the conversation about Pippi, but it didn't come. Her mother kicked off her shoes and rubbed her feet.

"Well, what are you going to do to Pippi?" Charlotte asked when she could no longer stand the suspense. "Make her live in the basement?"

Her mother looked amused. "Teach her not to chew phone cords," she said.

Charlotte felt her eyes water in gratitude. She wondered how she'd lived with her mother for ten years and not known what a nice person she was. As nice as Mrs. Arnold. Maybe nicer. Mrs. Arnold might not even like cats.

But thinking of the librarian made Charlotte sad again. It reminded her of all the trouble she was in at school. With Mrs. Arnold. With Miss Brown. With Tina and Laura and Jenny. Just thinking of Tina made her stomach churn. How could she ever sit at the dinner table across from Marie?

"What's the matter?" Mrs. Cheetham asked. From the kitchen came the sound of breaking glass. She rolled her eyes at Charlotte in a conspiratorial way, as if she knew the problems in this house were really due to Ruth and Marie. But that wasn't true, Charlotte thought unhappily. She was the one who told lies. Whoppers, too.

"Nothing," she said, but realized at once it was a lie. "Well—" She longed to confess. Maybe her mother could help her. Maybe her mother would even take them to New York to see a sticker factory. Look at how nice she'd been about Pippi and the phone cord.

"It's about my lies," she said vaguely, just to test her mother's reaction. "Like the one I told Mrs. Arnold, you know?"

Her mother nodded, her expression noncommittal.

"Well, now I can't go to the library anymore."

"Certainly you can," her mother said. "You just face up to what you've done. You tell Mrs. Arnold you're sorry."

Charlotte's hopes sank. Her mother sounded so sure of herself—so certain of what was right and wrong. Obviously, she was not going to drive Charlotte and a bunch of kids to New York to help cover up a lie.

Charlotte nodded as if her mother's suggestion were clearly reasonable. She could never do that in a million years, she thought.

91

*   *   *

At dinner, Charlotte avoided Marie's eyes. She concentrated hard on eating, examining each pea before she ate it, cutting her pork chop into tiny pieces and studying each one for signs of fat. Whenever Marie took a breath to speak, Charlotte's fingers trembled and peas fell off her fork.

"Do you know something about these peas that I don't?" her father asked, studying his own plate earnestly.

Charlotte shook her head and smiled self-consciously. Everyone watched her. "I guess I don't like peas anymore," she lied. She set down her fork. It was impossible to hold it with all those eyes upon her.

"Honestly, Charlotte?" her mother said, surprised. "We cooked these peas just for you, didn't we, Marie? Marie thought you couldn't face limas tonight."

Charlotte was startled into looking at her sister. Marie was smiling her mysterious smile.

"She said you had a rough day," Mrs. Cheetham continued. "Is that true?"

Charlotte cleared her throat and stared down at her peas. "I guess so," she said.

"Nothing serious, I hope," her father said, picking up his fork again. Charlotte saw, with relief, that they were all resuming dinner. Marie remained silent.

"Oh, no," Charlotte said, spearing an errant pea and popping it into her mouth. "Nothing serious." Miraculously, Marie didn't comment. Charlotte stared at her sister in wonder and gratitude.

The next two afternoons there were new teeth marks in what remained of the phone cord. Mrs. Cheetham held Pippi close to the telephone and rapped the cord harshly against the counter. "No," she said firmly each time. Pippi squirmed to get away and Charlotte could tell she understood. She probably just couldn't help herself. Charlotte knew exactly how she felt. Gradually though, Pippi learned. Whenever she came near the cord, her ears would perk up in excitement. She'd take one quick whiff and bound off the counter and down the cellar steps.

"It's a game," Charlotte's father said once at dinner after they'd watched this performance. "The cat likes to put a little excitement in her life, that's all." Everyone laughed. Charlotte thought she could understand a feeling like that perfectly. She just hoped Pippi's life never got as exciting as hers!

11

"My mother says she'll have to talk to your mother about the trip," Laura said. They were all busy trying to steal cookies from Jenny's bag. Stunned, Charlotte forgot to remove her hand and had it smashed by Jenny's fist.

"Ow," she said. She pulled her hand out and opened it. The cookie she'd been clutching was crushed to bits.

"Yummy," Tina said. "Eat up." She knocked Charlotte's hand upward toward her mouth so that cookie crumbs fell everywhere.

"My mom says she'll call your mother to find out the details."

"It's only to New York," Charlotte said weakly, pretending to be engrossed in brushing crumbs off her sweater. "Just tell her that."

"I know, but she wants to know where we're going exactly. And what time we'll be back."

Tina looked at Laura in disgust. "Your mother treats you like a baby," she said.

Laura shrugged. "I'm an only child. She likes me."

Tina sighed. "I guess mothers can like anything," she said, backing off from Laura's punch.

Charlotte, scarcely aware that the subject had changed, sought to recapture Laura's attention. "My mom works all the time," she pointed out. "It's really hard to get in touch with her." But they were gone, out to the playground to continue their chase.

Across the table, Annie's eyes were wide with fright. "Think of something," she whispered, as if the problem were hers and she were calling on Charlotte to solve it. "Quick."

Charlotte, lost in thought, wandered to the girls' room and then back to class. She was startled when a hand tugged at one of her braids as she passed the library. She'd been so preoccupied by her new humiliation that she'd forgotten her old one. It was Mrs. Arnold who bent down now to smile at her, resting her hand on Charlotte's head. Beneath the hand, Charlotte's ears began to burn.

"You haven't been to the library for such a long

time, Charlotte," the librarian said pleasantly. "How are you getting along without your Pippi books?"

Charlotte couldn't speak. She stood, stupidly, staring down at the blue and white specks in the tiles of the hallway. She could feel the blood throbbing in her neck. This must be the reddest she'd ever turned in her entire life.

"You aren't angry with me, are you?" Mrs. Arnold asked gently. Charlotte's mouth dropped open in astonishment. She looked into Mrs. Arnold's face and saw that she was sincere. Charlotte closed her mouth and shook her head vigorously. "Well good," the librarian said. "Come in and see me then, okay?"

Charlotte nodded and watched Mrs. Arnold walk off. What was going on? Hadn't Marie really told the librarian that she was a liar? Charlotte felt a surge of hope that vanished as rapidly as it came. Even if she hadn't, Charlotte would have to confess. She couldn't go on letting Mrs. Arnold think she had a baby brother.

Charlotte felt alarmingly close to tears again. Now she would *have* to go to the library. She approached her classroom and saw Tina and Jenny trading stickers in the far corner of the room. She imagined Laura's mom calling her mom after school. This was the kind of day you ended up

with when you told lies, she thought desperately.
It was like the electric chair for liars. She pulled
on her braids and wished she were a cat that
could flit from room to room and never have to
land anywhere.

12

Charlotte and Annie walked home slowly, plotting.

"Can't you say the factory burned down?" Annie suggested. "Or the lady died?"

Charlotte supposed it was worth a try. She would go home tonight and find out the factory had burned. Then she'd call Tina to tell her the news.

"I'll call Tina at five," she said. "My mother gets home at five-thirty. I'll say she just walked in with terrible news."

Annie nodded, her face earnest. "Call Laura first," she advised. "Before her mom calls you."

They wouldn't believe her, Charlotte knew. They'd never share cookies or stickers with her again. They'd never believe a word she said.

No one would. At least her mother wouldn't find out. She thought of how nice her mother had been about Pippi. All the while Charlotte had been tangled up in her big fat lie after she'd promised to stop lying.

"It might work," Annie said hopefully. Charlotte smiled at her friend gratefully and walked her right to her door.

It wasn't until she was at her own back door that Charlotte noticed her mother's car parked in the driveway. Her mother's car? She stared at it, bewildered. Her mother never came home at this time of day. Charlotte's panic returned. She'd have to call Laura *now*. Right this minute. She hurried in through the back doorway, to be greeted by her mother, who looked pale and sick.

"Hi, Charlotte," she said listlessly. "Home sick."

Charlotte stared at her mother. "You're never sick," she said feebly. "You're never home during the day." She watched as her mother searched the cupboards for vitamins and cough drops.

"Well, today I am," her mother replied, running her hand across Charlotte's head. "And I need you to do me a favor. Run to the store and buy a few oranges. I think I need fresh juice."

Charlotte swallowed hard and pulled out from beneath her mother's hand. "Can I go later?" she asked. "In a few minutes?"

Mrs. Cheetham shook her head and smiled wearily. "I'm on my way to bed," she pointed out. "Run do it now and then you're free of me. Be sure to get juice oranges."

Charlotte took the dollar her mother handed her and backed out the door. She'd hurry. Laura's mom wouldn't be calling in the afternoon. She probably knew Charlotte's mother worked. Charlotte ran all the way to the store and back again, lugging the bag of oranges. As soon as her mother went to bed, she'd call Laura. This day *must* be a full moon, she thought. It was the worst day in her entire life.

She handed the oranges and the change to her mother. Now she supposed she would have to wait until her mother squeezed oranges before she could use the phone in privacy.

But her mother was not squeezing oranges. She was standing in the middle of the kitchen, holding the bag, staring at Charlotte.

"Charlotte," she said. "I have just had a very strange phone call."

Charlotte froze. Her face began to tingle. This was it. She'd been walking down that long hallway to the electric chair, and now she was strapped in place. She couldn't move her eyes to look at her mother's face, but she didn't want to see it anyway.

"Would you like to explain to me about this trip we're all taking?" Mrs. Cheetham asked, her voice harsh and unfriendly.

Charlotte gulped. Her lower lip began to quiver. "I'm sorry," she whispered. She managed to glance at her mother's face, which looked ferocious. Where had that weak, sickly woman gone? she wondered fleetingly.

"Explain it to me," her mother said again. Harsher.

Charlotte began to cry. She sank into a chair at the table and buried her head in her arms, feeling that she would cry until there was nothing left inside her to cry about. Her sobs were loud and painful, bringing her sisters into the room.

"What now?" Ruth asked.

Charlotte felt someone bump the table and fall into the chair across from her. She looked up, through tears, and saw her mother's face swimming there.

"I'm waiting, Charlotte," her mother said quietly. Charlotte's sisters moved closer to the table. Her mother did not even ask them to leave, as she usually did. Charlotte had been so bad that the whole world was invited to know about it.

"I didn't do it on purpose," Charlotte gulped hopelessly. She knew her mother would never accept this, though in a way it was true. "They said I was full of it. They never believe me."

"What weren't they believing?"

"That you had a friend at a sticker factory," she said defensively, startling herself. What was she talking about? Her sisters laughed.

"I *don't* have a friend at a sticker factory," her mother said without a change of expression. "Why should they believe you? Why should anyone believe anything you say? You *are* 'full of it.' "

Charlotte's lip quivered again. Her mother looked as if she hated her. She sounded like a judge who would send her to jail and never think of her again. More than anything, right this minute Charlotte wanted her mother to love her.

"I wanted them to like me," she said honestly, beginning to cry again, but more quietly this time. She didn't even care that her sisters heard. Nothing seemed to matter except that she straighten out the lies in her head and win back her mother's love. "Everyone hates me. They think I'm weird." She hiccuped with emotion. "I am weird. I can't even help lying."

Her mother's expression softened. She reached across the table for Charlotte's hand. She was beginning to look sick again, and Charlotte took a moment to feel pity for her. How could she stand a daughter like her when she was sick?

"In the first place, Charlotte," her mother said

earnestly, "you can't make people like you by promising them things. Real friends like you for what you are. Do you think Laura and these other girls are going to stick by you now?"

Charlotte shook her head. She thought of Annie, who had accepted her lie and tried to help her out of it. Annie was a real friend. The only one she had.

"And in the second place, I think you *could* stop lying if you really wanted to."

"But I can't!" Charlotte protested. "I say lies before I know I'm going to say them!"

Her mother looked serious. "Then you have to learn to think about what you're saying before you say it. Remember how we had to teach Pippi not to chew the phone cord? She couldn't help herself—she was wild and impulsive, like your crazy ideas are. You have to learn to control them, that's all. You can't live in a world with other people and do or say whatever you please."

"I have to tame myself?" Charlotte said, amazed. Her sisters laughed again.

"Let's get a whip," Ruth suggested.

"You girls go in the other room," Mrs. Cheetham ordered. "And leave Charlotte alone."

Relief spread through Charlotte like a warm river. Her mother still loved her. She would do whatever it took to tame herself.

13

Charlotte sat on the living room rug, staring at the television set without really seeing. She was practicing being blank. Every time a thought came into her head, she slammed the door on it. If she couldn't think normal thoughts, she had decided, she wouldn't think at all. Hundreds of doors swung open, slammed shut, and swung open again. It seemed hopeless.

Pippi darted out from under the desk and headed in her direction, but at the last minute the cat changed her mind and veered off toward the dining room. Charlotte sighed. Pippi would never let her pet her, she thought unhappily, and went back to slamming doors.

Mrs. Cheetham, who was stretched out beneath a blanket on the sofa, laughed. "Pippi has her own little routine of sorts," she pointed out. "It's just not what you'd expect it to be, is it?"

"What do you mean?" Charlotte asked, grateful for the distraction.

"Well, for instance, she always comes through this room exactly the same way," Mrs. Cheetham explained. "Never right through the middle, which would be the simplest way to do it. She always goes behind the brown chair, up onto the table, across the mantle, along the back of the sofa, and under the desk. Sometimes she comes out from under the desk to sniff something, but she'll never come over from behind the chair. She's got to go through the whole number."

"She's nuts," Mr. Cheetham volunteered from behind his newspaper.

Charlotte realized her mother was right. Each of the times Pippi had come close to her had been after she'd made her trip through the room and ended up under the desk. She laughed.

"And when she eats," Mrs. Cheetham observed, "she never eats directly from her dish. She positions herself on the other side of the water dish so that she has to stretch across it."

"Tastes better that way," Mr. Cheetham said. "I tell you, this cat has a sense of adventure."

Mrs. Cheetham laughed. "She's an eccentric, that's for sure."

"What's that?" Charlotte asked, not certain from her mother's tone of voice whether that was a good thing to be or not.

Her mother smiled. "An eccentric is—someone who does things his own way. He's unusual."

Charlotte thought about it. "Is that good?" she asked, still not certain. Mr. and Mrs. Cheetham looked at each other in a strange way. Charlotte understood immediately that the concern had shifted from the cat to her.

"Am I an eccentric?" Charlotte asked anxiously. Maybe that explained why she was always doing weird things. Eccentrics probably couldn't keep their minds blank.

"Look, it's not something you worry about," her father said. "If you are, you are. You don't think about it."

"I don't know about that," Mrs. Cheetham said. "Maybe if you know it about yourself it makes you stop trying to be something you aren't. I was an eccentric at school. None of the girls were ever science majors."

Charlotte sat upright and stared at her mother. Her crooked teeth were eccentric, too. "Did you want to be like the other girls?" she asked.

Her mother smiled and didn't answer.

"Did you wish you weren't so weird?" Charlotte demanded. She feared her mother had started one of those stories she wasn't going to finish.

Mrs. Cheetham sighed and looked serious. "Yes, for a long time I guess I did. But then I became a scientist, and it was exciting and interesting and it was worth being considered weird. Now lots of women are scientists. I was simply a little before my time. You just have to be what you want to be."

"I wonder what I'll be," Charlotte asked, more of herself than anyone in the room. She wondered if she could possibly end up being something good enough to make up for these years of being weird.

"A writer," her father said without hesitation. "A teller of tall tales." Mr. Cheetham obviously had not been informed of Charlotte's latest experiments in the telling of tall tales.

Charlotte looked at her mother guiltily and was relieved to see her smiling vaguely into the distance. Maybe she hadn't heard.

"After all," her father continued, "you don't want to waste that wonderful imagination of yours."

Charlotte was suddenly thoughtful. A writer? "I could put my stories into books," she said, startled by the prospect. "Then they wouldn't be lies!" She looked at her father for confirmation.

She could stop slamming doors on all her good ideas!

"Exactly," he agreed. Charlotte felt a burst of excitement. She would write books like *Pippi Longstocking*. Why hadn't she thought of it before?

At that moment the cat shot into the room and stood still, her ears perked, ready to run off again at the first sign of attention from any of them.

"You little eccentric," Charlotte shouted. The cat charged between her legs and across the room, breaking her routine in playfulness. She stopped at the stairs and looked back at Charlotte, who knew that the outburst was the closest thing she'd had yet to a gesture of affection.

14

Charlotte buried her head under her quilt, trying to sleep. It was impossible. By now, everyone knew. Laura would have called Tina who would have called Jenny. They all would have laughed and gloated at how stupid she'd been. Tina wouldn't really kill her, of course. It would just feel like dying to have to face her.

And to have to face Mrs. Arnold! Charlotte kicked the covers from her, suddenly hot. Mrs. Arnold liked her. No one had *made* her come up to Charlotte in the hall and ask her to come back to the library. But that made it all the harder, Charlotte thought miserably, thrashing so hard her quilt slid onto the floor. Mrs. Arnold mattered and Tina didn't.

*　　*　　*

Annie was horrified by the news that Laura's mother had called. "Tina will kill you," she pointed out repeatedly on the way to school. Her own steps lagged, anticipating Charlotte's fate.

Charlotte was more preoccupied with her decision to confess to Mrs. Arnold. She imagined walking into the library. Each step she took along the sidewalk was a step toward Mrs. Arnold. Now she was there. She stopped. Mrs. Arnold was smiling as if nothing had happened. Charlotte tried to smile back.

"What are you stopping for?" Annie said. "Who are you smiling at like that? You're about to get killed, remember?"

Charlotte continued walking, embarrassed.

"Do you ever get mad at me when I lie?" she asked after they'd walked awhile in silence.

Annie thought it over. "Well, usually your lies are funny," she said. "I don't think I get mad at you. I'd only get really mad at you if you decided to be somebody else's best friend."

Charlotte looked at her gratefully. "I'd never do that," she said. "If you like someone, you like them forever, no matter what they do. Unless it's stealing or murder or something like that." Annie nodded in agreement. Charlotte realized that Annie had known this truth all along. "I'm not

111

going to lie anymore," she said fervently, wanting to be as good as her friend.

Annie accepted this news without comment. "Do you think I can come *today* and see Pippi?" she asked.

Charlotte nodded. "You'll have to look at her from a distance until she gets used to you."

"I wish I had my own cat," Annie sighed. "My mother laughs when I mention it."

Charlotte was sorry for her. "You can be Pippi's aunt," she suggested. "You can bring her presents at Christmas and stuff like that."

Annie brightened. "Catnip," she said. "Cats just love that. It makes them crazy."

Tina was waiting eagerly, her face like a storm cloud. Charlotte took a deep breath.

"Liar," Tina said, falling into step beside her. "Big fat liar. You are an imbecile, Charlotte Cheetham. You know that?" Charlotte felt her face flush scarlet. Rat, she thought in reply. Ignoramus. But she didn't say anything. "You got Laura and Jenny all excited. They were stupid enough to believe you. They actually thought you had a brain in your head."

Charlotte stopped walking. "I'm sorry," she mumbled, quieter than she intended. The words stuck in her throat.

112

Tina, when Charlotte looked up, appeared stunned. "What?" she said.

Charlotte cleared her throat. "I'm sorry I lied," she said.

Bewilderment crossed Tina's face, but she recovered. "Being sorry isn't good enough," she said. "You're still a jerk."

An eccentric, Charlotte thought, but she walked off without comment.

At ten o'clock, Charlotte asked for a library pass. She didn't like the way the teacher smiled when she handed it to her. She was tired of being smiled at and chuckled over.

But things were about to change. This was like the final chapter of a book, she decided, making her way slowly down the hall toward the library. She imagined her face peering off of a dust jacket with a bold-faced title: CHARLOTTE CHEETHAM, TELLER OF TALL TALES. How would she have the book end, if she were writing it?

Happily, of course. Mrs. Arnold would smile at her and say that she understood completely. Charlotte had never intended to lie. It was just something that happened. Charlotte's pace quickened in anticipation. Someday she might write that very book. It would be her autobiography.

Mrs. Arnold, alone in the library, had her back to the door. To Charlotte, her back looked a lot less understanding than her front. She shelved books methodically, arms moving up and down in a businesslike fashion, books sliding into place in neat, even rows. Her ponytail had disappeared into a knot at the back of her head that strongly resembled Mrs. Cheetham's. Charlotte felt a new burst of alarm. She'd come back another day, she thought hastily. Next month. It would be easier the older she got. But before she could back out the doorway, Mrs. Arnold caught a glimpse of her over her shoulder.

"Why, Charlotte," she said, forgetting the book she was about to shelve and turning around. Her eyes were still green and friendly, Charlotte saw with relief. And her hair, from the front, appeared exactly the same. Still, Charlotte did not know how she could possibly look into those eyes and say what she'd come to say. She'd been crazy to think she could.

"It's been very boring in here without you," Mrs. Arnold was saying. She set down her book and crossed the room. Charlotte watched her maneuver around desks and chairs, eliminating obstacles between the two of them one by one.

"Charlotte, you look absolutely terrified," Mrs. Arnold said. "What's wrong?"

114

Charlotte took a deep, shaky breath. She was conscious of being trapped in a doorway, within earshot of anyone passing by. "I told a lie," she began, but her voice emerged as a whisper. "I told a lie," she said again, this time more loudly than she'd intended. "About my mother's having a baby. You probably hate me."

Mrs. Arnold put her arm around Charlotte's shoulder and drew her into the library. She didn't look as if she hated her. "I could never hate you, Charlotte," she said. "You're a lovely little girl."

Charlotte shook her head vehemently. "I have told at least a million lies already in my life. Maybe more." It wasn't fair to let her go on thinking she was a "lovely little girl."

Mrs. Arnold laughed. Charlotte looked up, startled. "You have a lively imagination," the librarian said kindly. "You're sort of irrepressible, like Pippi. I don't think you mean to lie."

Charlotte was amazed. It was exactly what she'd imagined Mrs. Arnold saying! "I don't," she said gratefully. "And I'm going to stop lying. I'm going to be a writer instead."

Mrs. Arnold didn't look surprised. She simply nodded. "I'm sure you will," she said earnestly. "And I expect to have copies of all your books in this very library."

"I'll *give* you copies," Charlotte said eagerly.

"Signed ones that are worth lots of money." It was the least she could do for Mrs. Arnold, who had been so forgiving. "After all," she added, "this is sort of where I got my start." Baby Bill might even be the hero of her first novel. He would live by himself, like Pippi, and tell lies.

Mrs. Arnold smiled. "That's very true. I might have to give tours to all your fans."

Tours? What a wonderful idea! Charlotte looked around the room, surveying landmarks. She imagined Mrs. Arnold, a little older and more distinguished-looking, pointing out the spot where Charlotte Cheetham always stood to look at Pippi books. And here is where she waited in line to check them out. And there, in the corner, is the chair where Charlotte sat during free time to look at magazines. Mrs. Arnold might want to put a little gold plaque on the chair so that people wouldn't sit in it and wear it out.

Oh, yes! Charlotte thought happily. A little gold plaque that would read:

CHARLOTTE CHEETHAM
SAT HERE